POOR GIRL, RICH GIRL

Also by
JOHNNIECE MARSHALL WILSON:

Oh, Brother

Robin on His Own

POOR GIRL, RICH GIRL

Johnniece Marshall Wilson

AN
APPLE
PAPERBACK

SCHOLASTIC INC.
New York Toronto London Auckland Sydney

No part of this publication may be reproduced in whole or in part, or stored in a retrieval system, or transmitted in any form or by any means, electronic, mechanical, photocopying, recording, or otherwise, without written permission of the publisher. For information regarding permission, write to Scholastic Inc., 555 Broadway, New York, NY 10012.

ISBN 0-590-44733-5

12 11 10 9 8 7 6 5 4 3 2 1   5   4 5 6 7 8 9/9

Printed in the U.S.A.   40

With much, much love,
I dedicate this book to
my daughter, Tonya C. Wilson,
and to my siblings, Ella M. Long,
Jimmy L. Marshall, Robert Marshall,
Tom Marshall, Doris J. Webster

POOR GIRL,
RICH GIRL

ONE

I can remember a lot about the summer when I first got a job. But I have to go back to May, three weeks before school closed, to tell everything that happened.

That May morning when it all started, we were in the kitchen eating breakfast. April had been cold that year, but in May it warmed up some. Sunlight streamed in through the dining room window. I remember that, on account of April had been mostly overcast skies and icy rains. Things definitely started changing in the merry month of May.

I wanted to ask Mama and Daddy for money to buy contact lenses and one new outfit, and I wanted to catch them when they were together. Breakfast was the best time, I'd decided.

"Mama," I said.

But Mama was real sharp. She already knew what I was up to. I hadn't really dropped any hints, but I had told her that Leonardo da Vinci had come up with the original concept for contact lenses. Besides, she's real studious and reads all sorts of suspense thrillers.

She had her glasses on the top of her head, nestled in her thick black hair. Glasses, they say, are supposed to make you look studious. I think when they say that, they mean glasses that don't call attention to your eyes the way mine do. My glasses are real thick and have great big dark frames. The lenses make my eyes look extra large, like jumbo eggs. The lenses are as thick as the bottoms of pop bottles. I guess they're using thinner glass for pop bottles now, but you put two of the bottoms together, and you get a perfect picture of what my glasses look like. They make me look like the first alien to land on earth. A bug-eyed monster, I reckon.

While I was thinking about my glasses and trying to figure out a way to go on, Mama said, "Miranda, I've already told you we can't afford anything right now. Isn't that right, Mike?"

Mike is my father. Mama had wanted me to have a name that started with "M," like his. I guess she didn't think of Michelle, so she named me Miranda.

Daddy didn't answer, so Mama pulled her glasses out of her hair, set them on the very tip of her nose, and looked at my father over the tops of the lenses. "Mike — "

"But I don't want new clothes," I went on. "School is almost out for the summer." In the summer, I could live in cut-off jeans and an old ragged sweatshirt. I did want clothes, but I could wait until August for them. I took off my glasses and polished them on the corner of the tablecloth. Mama frowned. I smiled weakly and put them back on again.

Mama bit off a corner of her toast, chewed thoughtfully, then said, "Well, what do you want?"

"Contact lenses," I said, looking from Mama to Daddy. I guess I expected a drumroll or something. Their expressions didn't change. I picked up my toast and spread strawberry jam on it. Mama had made breakfast. It was delicious. Food always tastes better when someone else do the cooking.

"Now that's a little bit too much money," Mama said. "Isn't that right, Mike?"

My father still didn't answer. He sat across the table from Mama, calmly eating his oatmeal and reading the sports page he'd folded a thousand times so it'd be small enough to prop against the sugar bowl.

"I can get a pair and a spare for one hundred and forty dollars. And thirty dollars for the eye exam," I said. I couldn't eat. The piece of toast

3

I'd already bitten off and was trying to chew tasted like a cotton ball. I let the remainder plop down into my bowl of gooey oatmeal and pushed the whole thing toward the center of the table. "Just a little more than twice what my glasses cost."

"Mike?" Mama said again. "Tell her — "

Daddy still didn't say anything. He wears glasses, too. He stopped staring at the sports page long enough to push his glasses up on his nose. He turned the sports page over and went back to staring at it.

Mama pushed up her glasses and glared at my father, shook her head and said, "We all wear glasses. I think they're smart-looking. We're a family full of eggheads." She laughed out loud and slapped her palm on the table. The dishes rattled. Daddy's newspaper slipped off the sugar bowl. He picked it up, propped it again, and went on reading.

Egg-eyed eggheads, I thought. It wasn't that funny, but I said, "These are old and loose and the lenses are too thick. Kids at school tease me — "

"I told you to be careful with your things. Besides, I don't care what other people think."

"It isn't my fault they're broken. It's that dog." The Shephards lived next door in the house almost exactly like ours. They had the biggest dog in the world. He was bigger than a Shetland pony. I know because I rode a Shetland pony once when

I was a little kid. It wasn't nowhere near as big as the Shephards' dog.

"Miranda, I've told you, I think that dog just wants to play. You see how big he is. Other little dogs around here probably run from him."

"I don't blame them," I said.

"Stop interrupting. The Shephards aren't spry enough to keep up with a dog that size."

Opposite me, my father rustled the sports page, turned it over again. He looked at his watch and said, "You'd better hurry, or you'll be late for school. I've spoken with Shephard about that dog." I guess me and Mama had finally wakened Daddy.

"How can you ever get a pair of contact lenses 'round here?" I grumbled as I pushed back my chair. It slid easily across the slick tile floor. I got up. I clomped upstairs.

My room is just medium-sized and has a window on the far wall. There's a bureau next to the window. Just across from the window is my bed. I had already made it so I wouldn't have it to do after school. Across from the bed is my little red desk that Mama bought me from Goodwill. She'd painted it a kind of antique red to match my little red stereo. They'd given me the little red stereo for my birthday last September. That's one reason I thought they'd have money to buy me contacts. I hadn't even asked for a stereo. But on the other hand, back then, my father had had some money left over from when he used to sell insurance.

I kept my stereo on top of the bureau because there wasn't anywhere else to put it.

Sighing, I sat on the foot of my bed and stared at the stereo. On top of the bureau and flowing down to the floor were stacks and stacks of Teena's compact discs. Teena is my best friend. Ever since her house got burglarized in the early part of last spring, she's been keeping her CDs at my house. Thieves stole everything they could push, shove, and tote out of Teena's house. I wondered why they hadn't taken her CDs, too. Teena lived only a few blocks away, and I was a little scared that the burglars would come to my house next.

I got off the bed and started getting dressed. I turned on the radio. The little red stereo also had a CD player, a cassette player, and an AM-FM radio. I liked to listen to the radio in the mornings. But I couldn't see me spending my money on tapes and CDs. They changed them too much. Every week there was a new one. I would've spent a fortune.

The door to my room was closed. I guess my folks couldn't hear the music, but I didn't care either way.

Just then Daddy hollered, "Miranda, don't leave that radio blasting like that! Turn it off before you come downstairs."

6

I had finished dressing and was tying my shoelaces. I stopped what I was doing and turned the radio down, knocking a hundred of Teena's CDs to the floor in the process. One day, I was gonna have to clean up that mess.

After finishing tying my shoes, I grabbed Daddy's old genuine leather briefcase that I used as a book bag and crammed my books into it. The briefcase was left over from the days when Daddy sold insurance. It wasn't a large briefcase but one that looked something like a woman's purse, with my father's initials, M. M., embossed in gold. The briefcase was burgundy and my father's initials, which were also my own, were beginning to flake off. My parents, those two skinflints, had suggested I use the briefcase when I'd asked them for ten dollars to get a canvas book bag. I sighed and hefted the briefcase and went downstairs.

Since Daddy had recently opened his own business, he could leave when he got ready. He wasn't ready. He was still in his bathrobe. It was Monday, Mama's second day off that week. She worked as a dietitian in a hospital.

Going through the kitchen, I said, "See you," to my folks. And not in my nicest voice.

Daddy said, "Wait a minute, Miranda, honey. It's not that we don't want to get you anything, we can't right now. I've got a brand-new business, and we still have house payments. Your mother's been buying thrillers at Goodwill." He laughed when he said that, because Mama washed the covers of the books before she read them. Of course, that didn't stop her from buying a brand-new best-seller when she couldn't wait. Although that wasn't often.

My father went on: "We have to have a cushion of cash to see us through. The cushion's mighty thin right now."

"Daddy, I'm gonna be late for school," I said. I looked at them. They didn't look too much like folks who'd try to deceive me, I thought.

"Have a good day," they said in unison, like they were fraternal twins. I rolled my eyes. Not at them. They would've grounded me until the middle of the twenty-first century if they had seen.

At the kitchen door, I opened it and peeked out to see if the Shephards' Great Dane was frolicking on the sidewalk. If Teena'd lived close by, that dog never would've let the burglars get within an inch of her house.

I didn't see the dog, so it was safe to go out. I went out and along the walkway toward the bus stop.

Inhaling from relief, I looked around the neighborhood. I loved it. We lived on a tree-lined street with neat rows of single-family houses on both sides. All the houses looked alike, but some of them were trimmed in different colors. Ours was trimmed in white. That made the red bricks stand out really nice. The Shephards' house was trimmed in red. I felt that made it look drab. Just like a house the Shephards would live in with the great big old horse of a dog.

Moving closer to the bus stop, I kept looking back to see if I could see the Shephards' dog. I still didn't see him.

This last Monday in May was the kind of day that made you want to hum softly to yourself. It was perfect, especially since I didn't see the Great Dane. But while I was still creeping along to the bus stop, the Great Dane jumped out of some hedges near the corner house. I screamed and started to run. He started chasing me. He was so close, I could feel his hot breath on my legs. He didn't bark or anything, just trotted along after me like he knew for a fact that I was gonna end up as his breakfast.

I think sometimes how lucky I was that day. The bus screeched to a stop at the corner, just as the dog chased me to the bus stop. The doors creaked open and I leapt aboard.

"Looks like I got here in the nick of time," the driver said, and grinned at me.

I mumbled something and went to the middle of the bus and sat down. Looking out the window, I saw the Great Dane had parked himself on the curb, his tongue hanging out and his tail thumping on the sidewalk.

Boy! It was gonna be a rotten day.

When I got to school, it was too early to go in. They always made us wait outside the building until the last bell rang at eight twenty-five. I looked at my digital watch. It was eight-sixteen. I had nine whole minutes to kill. Other kids were milling around. Some kids were sitting on the steps. There wasn't room for me. Besides, it was those snooty kids everybody was trying to fit in with. You know, the ones who wore great clothes and got low grades. Luckily for me, Teena came along right then.

She was out of breath. She had obviously missed the bus. I wish she had been on the bus I rode to school. "Hello," Teena said.

"Hi," I said, glumly.

"Are you gonna get them?" she asked, meaning my contact lenses. I'd told her all about it.

I shook my head.

"Maybe you'll get a summer job." She slapped her books down on the concrete steps. We were standing in the entryway. "I'm going to work at my aunt's catering service. You can go down there. I bet she'll give you a job, too."

"Cooking?" I asked. "You already know I hate cooking." I wondered what she was going to say when I told her what else my mother had said.

"She'll just start you off grilling hot dogs and hamburgers," Teena said. "Even a little kid can do that."

"No thanks," I said. "Besides, I have to cook

at least three times a week at home now."

"How come?"

"Mama says I have to. She says I ought to learn how. So I won't have to practice on my husband when I get one."

Teena laughed, her white teeth flashing in the morning sun.

That made me mad. "For your information, I'm getting a husband who likes to cook."

"Okay. Okay," Teena said. "It's just funny. I can imagine your mother saying something like that. She's always saying funny things."

Teena picked up her books. I shifted my father's old leather briefcase to my left hand. The bell rang.

As we rushed into the building, Teena said, "You can get a job through the school. Didn't you see the notice posted on the bulletin board?"

There were bulletin boards all over the school. I yelled, "Which bulletin board?" I had to yell on account of the other kids were making so much noise going to their homerooms.

Somehow Teena and I got separated in the throng of kids. I saw Teena's hand go up over the heads of a flurry of kids. She pointed toward the main office, then disappeared in the crowded hallway.

In my homeroom, all the while the teacher was taking roll, I could barely sit still. I had to check that hallway bulletin board. I had to get one of those jobs. There was no other way. I could already see me wearing the contact lenses my own money had bought and paid for. I took off my glasses and studied them. I could already see me being as popular as a rock singer with four hits in the Top Ten. I was so deep in my fantasy, I almost didn't hear the bell ring signaling the end of homeroom.

TWO

My first-period class was on the third floor right down the hall from my homeroom. I didn't have enough time to zip down to the first floor and get back to my class.

I look back and wonder how I got through the three classes before lunch period. But somehow I made it.

At lunchtime, ordinarily, I'd meet Teena and we'd eat together. But that day, the last thing in the world I wanted to do was eat lunch. Instead, as soon as the bell rang ending general math — my third-period class — I jumped out of my seat and hied myself downstairs to the bulletin board in the main office hallway.

When I got there, I couldn't believe how many kids had the same idea I had. I couldn't even get close to the board because kids were standing around it, four-deep. I craned my neck, but the announcement poster was too far away. Even with my thick glasses, I could barely make out a word. The words I could see were blurred and elongated. It looked like hieroglyphics. I'd turned to leave when I saw Catriona Maryland come out of a counselor's office. I turned my back, feigning interest in what little I could see of the bulletin board, but I was already too late. Catriona had already seen me. Out of the corner of my eye, I saw her make her way toward me. Maybe she's just coming to read the bulletin board, I thought.

No such luck.

Catriona fitted in all the groups. But she and I simply couldn't get along. And it's always been like that, ever since we went to kindergarten together. I remember one day, the whole kindergarten class had sat on the floor, finger painting pictures. Catriona had walked on mine. Got paint all over the soles of her shoes. Our teacher had simply sat Catriona down and wiped the paint off. My picture had been ruined.

That was all a long time ago, but I do remember later, when we were in the fifth grade, our teacher always treated us special on our birthdays. I remember for my birthday that year, Mrs. Karsh had given me a copy of John Ruskin's *King of the Golden River*. When I left it in my desk until after recess, Catriona found it and tore the last page out. She scribbled on some of the pictures, too.

I thought now that we were older, she'd stop doing things like that, like getting on my nerves, but she hadn't.

Watching her walk toward me now, I wondered again if I should try to skulk away. I decided not to.

Catriona was taller than me. She had already developed a bust and wore clothing that showed this off. She had cut her hair. Her eyes were big and brown. She was light-skinned.

"Hello, there, Miranda," Catriona said, pretending she was glad to see me.

"Catriona — hello," I said.

"So, you're looking for a job? You could use one with that wardrobe. And those glasses. They remind me of a carp."

I don't know what she thought she was doing. There was nothing wrong with my outfit. I was wearing slacks and a tan T-shirt. Of course, Catriona was wearing an oversized designer blouse and matching skirt and vest.

I edged closer to the bulletin board. Catriona followed me. "Ain't no sense looking up there. I know, 'cause I've already got one of those jobs."

"How?" I asked. "The program won't start until the first of June."

"I've got connections," she said, and patted her

close-cut hair. "Oh, I've got to get on down to the cafe." She pronounced it *caff*. "Ta-ta, Miranda," she said over her shoulder as she left me there.

After she'd left, I realized that what she meant was that her father had connections. I knew she meant her father had pulled strings to get his daughter into the summer jobs program. Her father'd do something like that.

I sighed and just stood there until most of the kids had left. I went up close and read the notice. Actually, it was based on your annual household income. That meant I was sure to get a job. How much money could my father make in his brand-new business? And Mama couldn't've been making a fortune as a dietitian. That's what it sounded like this morning. They didn't have but a pittance. All both of them singing me their sad, sad song.

The bell rang. My stomach growled. I realized I'd stood in the corridor for my entire lunch period. I was starving. I hadn't eaten my oatmeal, or my strawberry jam-smeared toast, either. I was hungry.

I went to the vending machine at the end of the hallway and bought a Mounds candy bar, risking being late for my fifth-period class.

I leaned against the machine and ripped the paper from the candy bar. I ate most of it right there, realizing that if Mama found out, she'd have a conniption fit, with her being a dietitian and all. But I didn't care. Food is always good when sombody else do the cooking, or in this case, candy-making, I thought as I raced out of a side door so I wouldn't be late for gym.

Gym isn't my favorite class. I'm only taking it because the Board of Education says I have to. All that square dancing and basketball playing — one year, we even played touch football — can be left up to the ones who like that sort of thing.

I liked gym about as much as I liked cooking. Besides, I got enough exercise ducking and dodging the Shephards' Great Dane. I had been running from the dog for almost two years now, ever since we moved in next door to the Shephards. In August, it would be two years. I thought he'd be used to me by now, or the Shephards would've moved. But that's another thing I would learn that summer — things hardly ever turn out the way you want them to.

THREE

That afternoon when the two-fifty bell rang, I was already halfway out the door. In a way, I'm kind of ashamed of what I did, all because I wanted to be first. The only thing I could think to do was to go to the bookcases at the front of the room and pretend that I was looking for a book to read. Mrs. DeRoy loved that. She went into orbit anytime she saw a kid up there looking through the books. I mean I really pretended well that afternoon.

Like I say, the two-fifty bell rang. Throngs of kids leapt out of their seats. Books fell and were picked up. Papers were shuffled. A flurry of kids streamed out into the hallway. I heard their clatter and saw all this over my shoulder as I sped down the hall and down the stairs to Mrs. Storm's office.

I wasn't first, sad to say. In spite of everything, there were already a few kids in the hall lined up in front of me. I took my place on line and waited.

Mrs. Storm came out of her office and handed us applications and told us to fill them in and to be quiet.

Using a felt-tipped marker and bold strokes, I filled mine out. I didn't know it then, but it was just the first of many that I would have to fill out between now and the end of summer.

Satisfied that I had completed the application to the best of my ability, I still had to wait my turn before being interviewed.

I waited out in the hallway for what seemed like a long, long time. Only it might not've been. Finally Mrs. Storm stuck her head around the door and said, "Miranda — "

I went into the office and stood in front of her desk.

"Your application seems to be in order," Mrs. Storm told me. "I'll have to give you an appointment to bring in financial information from your parents." She wrote me a pass to get out of English class a week later at two o'clock. I slipped it into my purse, thanked her, and then went out. I closed her office door gently behind me.

Things were looking up. I had a good feeling about getting a summer job. And all the time I'd been worried about what Catriona'd told me. Now, I thought, all I have to do is get home without being bothered by the Shephards' Great Dane.

At home, I went to the kitchen. I tossed my books on the table and went to the fridge to get a snack. Before I could open the fridge door, I saw Mama's note. It was stuck on the fridge door with one of those little magnets that looked like a tiny bunch of Tokay grapes. She'd written the note on a pad she'd gotten from the hospital. At the top of the note paper was an ad for some product to aid digestion.

Using a lot of unnecessary loops and rattails, Mama'd scrawled:

Miranda —
   It's your day to cook. Prepare the food on the bottom shelf in the fridge.
                    Happy cooking,
                 Justine Moses, AKA Mama

I crumpled the note and tossed it into the kitchen garbage can. I sighed and kind of wondered why the Great Dane hadn't chased me. Then I would've had a good reason not to cook. But now there wasn't anything I could do about that. Mama was probably down at Goodwill looking over their books. She could get lost for a whole day when she went book browsing — forget all about the time and leave me and Daddy to fend for ourselves.

I opened the refrigerator. On the bottom shelf were some pork chops and cabbage. Mama had already cut the cabbage for me. Only thing, I didn't know what to cook first, so I threw everything into pots and pans and got it to cooking at once. Everything at the same time.

While the pork chops simmered in a pan and the cabbage boiled, I turned on the oven to preheat it and began mixing batter for corn muffins. Mama wouldn't buy those little packs of mix where all you had to do was add water. She'd said, "I can't give my family that." Good thing I had already learned a little about making muffins by watching Mama. I had never taken Home Ec, and I wasn't about to take it unless the Board of Education said I had to. Like gym.

I got everything to simmering and sputtering and I went and started doing my homework while all this stuff was cooking.

I opened my father's old geniune leather briefcase that I was using for a book bag and pulled out my history book. That's one of the reasons I don't like to cook. What do you do while the food's cooking? After all, a watched pot never boils. But now, I could at least study for my World History discussion. We were going to discuss Greek history on Tuesday.

I guess Greek history has a way of creeping up

on you and making you forget where you are and what you're doing. For a while there, I thought I was off in the Greek Isles, not in my own kitchen preparing dinner. Although I smelled some strange aroma, I kept right on reading. I sniffed. Then I realized what it was.

"Good grief!" I yelled. "Dinner's burning!" I jumped up and ran over to the stove.

The kitchen was very smoky. And was getting smokier by the second. Tears stung my eyes. I gagged and coughed. I was coughing so hard, I could barely turn off the stove.

Groping and trying not to burn myself, I finally managed to turn the fire off. Actually, I didn't turn the fire off. Rice water boiling out of the pot had already put out the fire. I turned the burner off so the house wouldn't get full of gas fumes.

I felt awful that I'd burned the rice. My father loved rice.

Even after I'd set the steaming pot into the sink, it went right on hissing and sputtering. The scent of scorched rice was still choking me. I bet you could smell it all over the neighborhood. It was thick enough to cut inside the house.

Mama kept aprons and hot pads and dish towels in a drawer next to the sink. I opened the drawer and found two oven mitts and slipped them on. I lifted the pot of rice and held it to the light from the kitchen window to see what I could salvage. The pot handle was hot even through the oven mitts. I turned on the cold water and filled the pot. Steam billowed up out of the mess and seared my left arm.

"Ouch!" I yanked the oven mitts off and fled down the hall to the bathroom.

There was a tube of ointment in the medicine cabinet. I got it, uncapped it, and smeared some on the burned spot. It was soothing, like ice.

Back in the kitchen, there was so much steam, my glasses fogged up. I snatched them off and wiped them on my apron. I opened the kitchen window over the sink. It didn't take long for the smoke to go out. The smell was still there, however. Now, I knew for a fact the whole neighborhood would know I'd burned dinner.

After the smoke cleared out, I scraped the top part of the rice into another pot, filled it, then started it cooking over a much lower flame.

I started to throw Mama's burnt pot away, but I thought if I kept it and let her see it, she wouldn't want me to cook again. The bottom of the pot was covered with about a cup of rice burned so black it looked like flecks of charcoal. I didn't scrape any of that out. Mama had to see it.

While the rice was simmering slowly and the cabbage was cooking, I finished the pork chops and turned them onto a meat platter. Then it was time to make gravy.

I chopped onion and put it into the skillet where I'd fried the pork chops. After they'd cooked about five minutes, I put in flour, browned that, then poured in a cup of water. I didn't turn the fire low because it wasn't boiling yet. I left the food there and went back to my Greek history.

Luckily for me, the gravy didn't burn while I was studying. It just got too dry. I could lift it out of the pan with a spatula like it was a load of bread. The next batch I made, I stood there and watched like a hawk.

I had hardly got the table set before I heard Mama and Daddy pull into the driveway. A glance at the clock on the wall above the table told me it was five-forty. I dashed across the kitchen and got an apple pie out of the fridge and stuck it into the oven right beside the pan with the corn muffins in it. The muffins looked great; they were just lightly browned. Mama would love them, especially if they tasted at least as good as they looked.

Mama had baked the apple pie the other day, and we just hadn't gotten around to eating it. Warm apple pie is always good. It was really perfuming up the kitchen by the time we sat down to dinner. I'd fixed the table real nice. I'd scooped the muffins out of the pan, and they were in a bun basket in the center of the table. You couldn't even smell burned rice at all.

"How was school?" Daddy asked, shaking his napkin and spreading it across his lap.

"Great! I'm going to get a job through the

school. They had some posted on the bulletin board. I signed up. I'm gonna buy my own contact lenses now."

"That's wonderful, Miranda," Mama said, smiling. Her eyes lit up behind her heavy-framed round eyeglasses. "What kind of job?"

"I don't know yet. They'll start assigning them next week."

"Your gravy is delicious," Daddy told me. "It's just the right consistency. Not too thin, not too thick. Is that apple pie I smell?"

I got up and got the pie out of the oven. I hadn't looked at the pie since I'd taken the muffins out. Good thing Daddy said something. All I was smelling were a lot of different foods all blended together.

I turned off the oven and set the pie on top of the stove. I sliced it and placed the slices on bread plates. I carried these to the table.

"Is this the same pie I baked the other day?" Mama asked.

"Yes. I could never bake like this," I replied.

"When you stop burning up pots, you'll be able to cook like this." Mama cut off a forkful of pie and tasted it. "All the seasonings' gone through it. Tastes good now."

"I think it tastes great," I said. "Especially since I didn't have to bake it. Food is always good when somebody else do the cooking."

Mama laughed. "You're always saying that, but

with you practicing, you're going to be a great cook. Isn't that right, Mike?"

In my dreams, I thought, but what I said was, "Thanks." Daddy just helped himself to more gravy. Good thing he was thin and could eat anything he wanted to.

After I'd cleaned the kitchen, I got ready to type my science essay. I had to write a paper on the ways mankind uses limestone. Teena had come over and was lying on the floor, doing her algebra homework. She'd brought a new CD, and it was playing softly on my little red stereo.

"Miranda, I gotta turn this up. This is my favorite song. Besides, your typing's drowning out the music." She got up and went over and turned up the sound. "You know I can't do algebra without music." She sprawled on the floor again. "On the other hand, I can't do algebra with music, either." She scratched out some problems she'd done incorrectly, balled up the sheet, and started a new page.

I laughed.

Teena said, "Girl, that ain't funny. This is the weirdest math in the world."

"How come you're taking it if you don't like it?"

"I guess 'cause I want to go to college."

"You could've taken general math."

"I will. In tenth grade. I've got to take geometry

in eleventh. I hear it's even weirder than algebra. But maybe I'll be able to make some sense outta all those lines and angles. On the other hand, looks like algebra oughta be easy. It ain't nothing but a lotta alphabets. Music is, too, but I didn't master that. 'Member when we went out for the band?"

"How can I forget?" I said, and laughed again. One September, Teena just know who'd be the greatest trumpet player in the world. And I just knew being a drummer was as easy as it looked. All that noise had almost driven me crazy. Not to mention what it did to Mama and Daddy. Because I did practice. Every chance I got, I practiced like my life depended on it. In the end, I had given up and joined the Reading Club.

All that was ancient history now. What I wanted more than anything else on earth was to get a summer job.

Teena was saying, "Did you finish reading that novel?"

"Not yet. I'm going to, even if I have to read all weekend."

"How many pages in that book anyhow?"

"Nine hundred or so," I said, and got the book off the corner of my desk and held it so she could see it.

"You *will* be reading all weekend. Not me. I'm

reading a thinner book. Besides, I have to start working not only weekends, but mornings and after school at Aunt Delight's."

"Cook something good, hear," I told her.

"I cook all the time at home. But my aunt'll probably just have me making hot dogs and hamburgers. 'Specially since she put in that walk-up window."

Teena looked at her watch. "I'd better get outta here before it gets dark." She stacked her books and stood up. She handed me a sheet of paper. "You're good at algebra. Check this for me. You can tell me how bad it is tomorrow." She moved toward the door. "I hope you get the kind of job you want. Or else something pretty close to it. I heard 'round school that a lotta kids are gonna get cut out of the program. See you."

"Catch the early bus tomorrow," I said. I started to get up.

"You don't need to see me out. I been coming over here since forever." She grinned and opened my room door and went out.

From downstairs, I heard Teena say good night to my folks. A short time later, the front door clicked shut.

I got up and closed my room door and turned the stereo to an all-music station. I went back to my desk and sat down. I still had a lot of work to finish for the semester before I could concentrate on working all summer for real money. I looked at the big book I'd chosen to read for English. I'd only read a hundred pages or so. I swung my legs back under my desk and started back to typing my science essay.

FOUR

All through the next few days, I could hardly get through my classes. I wanted a summer job so bad. I had taken to skipping lunch and going to the library to read my book so I wouldn't have to spend all lunch period thinking about getting a job or not getting one. This way, I killed two birds with one stone. I finished my novel, and I didn't have to think. I didn't want to have to think about what Teena'd said, especially: ". . . a lotta kids are gonna get cut out of the program." I could still hear her words, although she'd said them almost three days before.

Going to classes was hard enough. I could barely wait for Thursday so I could keep my appointment with Mrs. Storm and get it over with.

On Wednesday, I had been in the library reading and had stayed too long. The chapter I'd been reading was so interesting that I didn't even hear the bell signaling the end of fourth period. The librarian came over to my table and asked me didn't I have a fifth-period class. I looked at my watch and saw that we were almost ten minutes into fifth period.

I hastily gathered my things and jumped up. Gripping my books tightly in my arms, I raced for the stairs. But I couldn't go to my fifth-period class, World History. My stomach was grumbling and rumbling like mad. My knees buckled from hunger. I realized I hadn't eaten since supper the night before. I went to the vending machine and got a Mounds and munched on it on the way to World History. Maybe that'd take away the growling in my stomach until I got home, I thought.

Naturally it was very late by the time I got to my class. And I still hadn't finished my candy bar. I was still munching on it when I got to my class. I opened the door and went in.

Mrs. Beadle looked at me and frowned but went on with her lecture as I skulked past her to my desk.

I sat down and opened my history book and searched for the proper place. Still chewing on the last bit of candy at the same time.

"Can anyone tell me where the island of Patmos is?" Mrs. Beadle asked. She stood there looking around the class, waiting for a hand to go up. I sat at my desk, flipping through the history book and chewing flakes of coconut. I looked around the room. Mrs. Beadle kept on looking, too, hopefully. I knew the answer but couldn't raise my hand because my mouth was full of candy.

"Okay, Catriona," Mrs. Beadle said. She was so delighted that someone had volunteered that she grinned like a hyena. A curly wisp of salt-and-pepper hair fell into her eye.

Catriona rose. She seemed even taller as she stood in the aisle next to her desk. Her desk was in the row one over from mine. She leaned with one hand on the back of my chair.

"The island of Patmos is in the Aegean Sea, off the coast of Greece. That's where St. John the Revelator wrote the Book of Revelations," Catriona said, looking down at me, a smirk on her face. She leaned down, her mouth level with my ear. She whispered, "Well, did you get a job?"

I ignored her question as I stared up at her. She had put an S on Revelation. You could still hear it hissing all through the room.

Mrs. Beadle said, "That's very good, Catriona. And thanks for the Biblical history lesson. Only a preacher's daughter would know that. Or someone who's done her homework." She grinned at Catriona like Catriona was her own daughter and had just handed Mrs. Beadle a report card full of A's.

Still chewing on candy, I raised my hand.

"You're joining us, Miranda. Good. When you've finished chewing, tell us what's on your mind."

"There's no S on Revelation," I said. When Catriona'd said it, it sounded like someone'd turned on a faucet in the room. Or maybe a snake was slithering about, hissing as it went.

An annoyed frown creased Mrs. Beadle's forehead. But she nodded and said, "You're right, Miranda. Thank you. I believe I did hear the S."

Catriona slunk down in her seat. When she looked at me, she rolled her eyes. I didn't care. I stuck my tongue out at her and grinned almost as wide as Mrs. Beadle had.

Twenty minutes later, the bell rang, ending World History. Catriona was usually the first one out the door since she was the tallest and had the longest legs, I guess, but she stayed in her seat and waited until I'd stacked my books and gathered them up into my arms.

Just as I was about to stand, she rose and stood opposite me. "You've got a smart mouth," she hissed at me, still sounding snaky.

I smiled and scooted between the front of my desk and the chair in front of it. Catriona scooted around in front of me and blocked my way. I peered over Catriona's shoulder at Mrs. Beadle, but Mrs. Beadle was busy in the corner near her desk, her back to Catriona and me.

"Although it might be the last thing that I do,

I'm gonna get even with you, Miranda Moses," Catriona spat at me.

"What — what did I do?" I asked innocently, knowing full well that Catriona hadn't liked me correcting her.

"You — you're just too smart-alecky. You get on my last nerves. You — " All the time she was shaking a long, bony, brown finger in my face. I was resisting the urge to bite it in two.

"I've got to go," I said.

"Mrs. Storm did tell me last week that I've got one of those jobs. If you on your way to see about one, I hope they're all gone."

Before I could answer, Catriona had snatched her books from her desk and had flounced out into the hallway.

I glanced at Mrs. Beadle. She was sitting in her desk chair, reared back and talking on the phone. I switched my books to my left arm and walked out of the room.

FIVE

The candy bar didn't do my stomach a world of good. It was still empty and let me know it by roaring like a caged tiger. A hungry caged tiger. Now I had excitement *and* hunger to worry about.

On the first floor, I could still smell the aroma of what they'd served for lunch, coming out of the cafeteria. It smelled like some kind of pasta. And I smelled broccoli, my favorite vegetable. My mouth watered. It wasn't good to miss lunch the way I'd done. Besides, food is always good when somebody else do the cooking.

A hunger pang struck me in the pit of my stomach as I got closer to Mrs. Storm's office and out of range of the cafeteria smells. I sighed, adjusted my glasses, then knocked on Mrs. Storm's door.

"Come in," she said. Her voice seemed to ricochet off the frosted glass pane in the door. I'm almost positive that the glass trembled.

I turned the knob, opened the door, and went inside. Mrs. Storm's office is just what you'd expect a school office to be. A row of battered black filing cabinets stood against one wall. The walls were cream-colored, and the floors were cracked dark tiles; some of them puckered where a lot of people had walked.

Mrs. Storm was a chunky little woman, dwarfed behind the big metal desk where she sat. The desk was painted to match the filing cabinets.

"Miranda?" she said as I approached her desk.

"Yes," I said. I was trying not to stare. Mrs. Storm's hair was lopped off at about the same length as Catriona's. Mrs. Storm was the kind of person you see once and you don't forget. She wore thick white-framed eyeglasses. The lenses must've been thicker than mine. And she did look studious. Her face was fat and made her look like some kind of bird. When I noticed the red scarf barely sticking out of the neck of her dress, I knew what kind of bird she reminded me of: a woodpecker. A chubby woodpecker.

I started checking out the things on the top of her desk. No desk blotter, just an oversized piece of construction paper. The thing that caught my eye was the big thick book resting on the sheet of construction paper. She was reading the same book that I was reading for my English class. I was envious 'cause she was almost through with it. Although I'd read all weekend and had given up a lot of lunch periods, I hadn't cut a dent in the nine hundred pages. "I'm Miranda Moses," I said again.

There was a bookmark on the green sheet of paper. She took it up and marked her place. She closed the book but held onto it. I said, "Is that a good book?"

She smiled. "Sure is. I can't seem to put it down. It's written by my favorite author. Do you like to read, Miranda?"

"Yes." I didn't see any need to tell her that I was reading the same novel.

Mrs. Storm put the book on the corner of the desk. "Sit down."

There was a chair to the left of the desk. I set my books on the lowest of the filing cabinets and sat down.

"Since you're one of our better students, I hope I can get you a job in an office."

"That'll be nice," I said.

She opened my file. "Tell me, did you bring your family's financial records?"

I fished them out of my purse and handed them to her. She looked them over, said, "Hmmm," then set them on the desk as she copied a lot of figures and added them up. I could see my job application sticking out from under the papers she was scribbling on. I could tell because of my large handwriting. It was also done with a black felt-tipped pen.

Mrs. Storm furrowed her brow, picked up my application, and read it over. When she'd finished, she put the application down and laced her fingers together. She looked at me over her fingers for a long, long time. It was a look of pity. A look that made me think I was gonna fall off the face of the earth. Outside the window, a cloud covered the sun and darkened the room.

Mrs. Storm unlaced her fingers, then laced them again. She opened her birdlike mouth. It made her look like a baby bird about to take a worm from its mother's beak. But Mrs. Storm closed her mouth again, then opened it and said, "Miranda, I hate to have to tell you this, but you don't qualify for our summer jobs program. Your mother earns too much money. Too much for three people."

Nervously, I laughed, unsure of what I should say, what I should do. "There must be some kind of mistake," I said, lamely.

It was Mrs. Storm's turn to give a nervous little laugh. That's when I should've stood, should've gone out of her office, but I didn't. There was some kind of mistake. There had to be. We didn't have any money at all. Slowly, I eased out of the chair. My glasses chose that moment to slide down my nose. I pushed them up, thinking: We didn't have any money at all. If we did, my folks would've bought me contact lenses.

I stared at Mrs. Storm. This woman must be crazy. My folks just told me last week that we didn't have any money. That we hardly had two nickels to rub together. We didn't have any extra money for movies and records and such like. My last winter's coat had set Mama and Daddy back a pretty penny. Not to mention what the little red stereo must've cost them. If we had had money, I would've bought CDs, like Teena. At least, if I'd wanted to. What kind of mixed-up place was the world anyhow?

Mrs. Storm said, "I wish that there was something else I could do." She unlaced her fingers again and spread her arms in a helpless gesture. But all it did was make her look more like a bird, like she could really fly off somewhere. "If it's any consolation, your academic record is above reproach. You'll find something."

"Thank you just the same," I said. I got up and got my books off the filing cabinet. I wanted to get out of there. Mrs. Storm's office suddenly felt hotter than a July dog day; hotter than a blast furnace. My face burned. From where I stood, the door was only about four feet — six feet, tops — but it seemed like a mile. At last, I made it to the door and out. I closed the door. I didn't slam it, although I wanted to. I didn't stop to think about what to do or where to go. I raced out of the building like the hallways were on fire. Fire and flames were chasing me but not quite catching me. I hadn't fallen off the face of the earth — it just felt like I had.

In the corridor, I started up the stairs to my last-period class, but I couldn't face anyone. Not yet. Even my glasses were against me. They felt like they weighed a ton. I yanked them off and ran downstairs, headlong into the street.

Without my glasses, I couldn't see a thing. That didn't stop me from moving along on instinct.

Mama was gonna have to explain this to me. If they had some money, they should've said so. I didn't know what was going on. And Mama seemed so proud when I said I'd get a job.

How was I going to tell Teena this?

How could Catriona get a job and I couldn't? The way she dressed, her family looked like they had more money than a bank.

I raced around blind — literally — 'cause I hadn't bothered to put my glasses on again.

At the curb, I heard rather than saw cars barreling along the street. I started to cross against the light. It was a shining red blur without my glasses. A driver angrily honked and squealed to a stop. I waited, frozen to the spot, expecting cold steel to smash my body, but it didn't. The driver yelled something out the window, then scratched off real fast. I could smell burning rubber in the air.

I knew I had to put my glasses on if I wanted to get home in one piece. I wiped my eyes on the heels of my hands and fished my glasses out of my purse. I put them on and went home.

I was still too stunned to do anything except sit on the side of my bed, facing the closed and locked door. I kept looking back at my little red stereo, but I wouldn't get up and turn it on.

When Mama came home at three-twenty, I was still sitting on my bed. Evidently I hadn't made a sound. She came upstairs and took a bath and changed. I heard her running water and opening drawers. She went downstairs again. It was her day to cook, and she started that around four o'clock.

She never would've known I was home if the phone hadn't've rung. I got up and answered it. It was already on the landing just outside my door. I didn't care that she knew I was home or not. I just didn't feel like having her ask me a thousand questions.

Teena was on the phone. I told her I'd call her back and hung up before she said anything.

A few minutes later, Mama hollered upstairs and said, "Miranda, is that you?"

"No. It's your friendly neighborhood burglar," I said, but not loud enough for her to hear. Who did she expect it to be? She knew Daddy was out there making money and stashing it somewhere.

Mama came upstairs and turned my doorknob.

Of course, it didn't open. "Miranda —"

I stayed still.

"Open the door, honey."

I didn't move. I didn't answer.

"Listen, baby," Mama said from the other side of the door. "Something's happened. You've been home a long time —"

What was she, psychic? I thought, but said nothing.

"Miranda," Mama said again. "Let me in."

I got up and turned on the radio. Even as mad as I was, I still didn't like it loud. But it was loud enough. It almost drowned out Mama's voice.

She raised her voice over the radio. "Did somebody hurt your feelings?"

"No!" I yelled.

"Did you get suspended?"

"No."

"Please let me in."

She was beginning to sound like the big bad wolf trying to get into the three little pigs' houses. I almost laughed. Instead, I got up and let her in.

After I'd unlocked the door, I came back and sprawled across my bed. Mama came in and sat next to me. She stroked my hair. I told her what'd happened.

"You and Daddy could've said what was going on. It was so embarrassing to hear Mrs. Storm say we had *too* much money."

"Honey, we didn't lie to you. Look, there's two kinds of money. Money that's real and money that's on paper."

"Huh?"

"I'm explaining this badly, aren't I?"

"You can say that again."

She caught my hair up and twisted it, then smoothed it out only to twist it again. I kind of wished I hadn't let her in.

"I don't know what kind of program they have down at your school, but I'm assuming they're dealing with grosses, not net. Net is the real money. The money you're allowed to spend from your earnings. So much is taken for Social Security, so much for hospitalization, another sum for federal taxes, state taxes, local taxes, and so on.

"Let's say someone makes a thousand dollars a month. They'll bring home around four-thirty, two times a month. Four hundred thirty dollars two times a month is very little money. That's why you can make a lot and still not make much money."

I raised my head and looked at her. While Mrs. Storm had been figuring out my parents' income, she'd mumbled stuff to herself like gross and net and other things I didn't understand.

"Do you understand, honey?"

"I — I guess so."

"We'll find you a job somewhere."

I didn't say anything. Mama got up to go see about dinner. I stayed on the bed, lying on my stomach and staring at the floor.

At the door, Mama turned and said, "Don't stay up here moping. You'll make yourself sick."

"I'm already too upset to do anything," I told her. "And I'm never going back to that school. What's the use?"

Mama said nothing. I went on: "All I wanted was a lousy pair of contact lenses." I took off my glasses and looked at them. "I could've even gotten a couple new outfits. All my clothes threadbare —"

"No, they're not," Mama said, twisting the doorknob. "There must be some fast food restaurants where you can get a job."

"Mama, you haven't heard a word I said. You know I don't like to cook. I don't even wanna be around food unless I'm eating it."

"Miranda, don't use that tone of voice with me. You've got to get a job doing something. Especially since you say you want one so bad. I thought you wanted to earn some money. Going to look for a job just at your school does not constitute looking for work."

"What am I going to do?" I said more to myself than to Mama.

"You don't have to be a cook in a fast food restaurant. You can be a cashier."

"I can't do that, neither." I couldn't believe my

mother. I couldn't muster enough courage to stand up in front of my classmates and give an oral book report, and she was telling me I could be a cashier. If I wasn't so nervous, I'd at least give an oral book report. Then my teacher couldn't take off points for bad writing.

"Okay, Mama, I'm going to find something. It's going to be something I like. And I'm going to work all summer."

Mama turned the doorknob a few more turns, then went downstairs to check on dinner.

Six

On Friday, I was still mad. Still mad at Mama and still mad at my school, but I got up and got dressed and went back to school. I know I said I wasn't going, but it was just like Mama said, I couldn't sit around moping. Besides, I've never heard of anybody going to college without graduating high school except William Faulkner and Sammy Davis, Jr.

At school, I tried to avoid everybody except Teena. I felt bad about not calling her back. When I did see her, she was real sympathetic and kept telling me about Delightful Catering.

I kept saying "no thanks," but that's never stopped Teena from doing or saying anything she wanted. Maybe that's why I liked her so much, although I did think she ought to come over and pick up her CDs.

"Know what?" Teena said.

"No. What?"

"The teachers have an in-service day on Tuesday."

"We can find me a job then," I finished for her. We laughed.

All day at school, the hallways were buzzing with other kids talking about their new summer jobs. I could barely get through the day. When the bell rang at two-fifty, I was glad to leave, glad to go home. At least, I'd read some of that book. I had managed another fifty pages last night. I could try for another fifty tonight if the Shephards' Great Dane didn't gobble me up before I got home.

Luckily, the dog wasn't out. I skulked along the tree-lined street and got home safe and sound.

In my room, I pitched Daddy's old genuine leather briefcase on my desk so hard that it jarred the whole room. Some of Teena's CDs slid off the chest of drawers, but I didn't care. I grabbed the novel, sprawled across the bed, and started reading.

I read all weekend and the next week. I read on my lunch period and again on the bus coming home from school. I was finally starting to cut a dent in the nine hundred-odd pages. There were only two times that I stopped reading. Once when I had to cook dinner, and again when Mama and

I drove to Goodwill to buy a used suspense thriller. We had to hurry because it was twelve minutes to six, and they closed at six. I was only going to take my mind off things.

Amid the musty old stalls at Goodwill, Mama said, "It's been so long since I had a brand-new book. They have nothing here but romance novels. Wall-to-wall romance novels. They don't have the suspense I'm looking for." She selected a couple of books and went to the cashier's stand. Mama paid for the books and we left.

It was still light outside, and I managed to read a page and a half while we were driving home. As I was getting out of the car, I made a mental note that when I did get a job, I'd get Mama a brand-new hardcover suspense thriller. Of course, she didn't deserve it. I was still mad at her because she wanted me to take any old job, even one I hated.

Monday after school, I didn't bother about reading the novel. There was something else I wanted to read. So I sprawled across my bed until four o'clock, resting my eyes. At four o'clock, it came. You could set your watch by Alex, the paperboy. They say he has another route across town, but at four o'clock, he was throwing our paper up against the screen door.

As soon as I heard the paper strike the door, I hopped off the bed and raced downstairs to get it. He had it rolled into a tomahawk and creased like crazy. I undid it and threw the sports page into the big blue easy chair by the window in the living room so Daddy'd be sure to see it first thing when he got home. He didn't care what we did with the rest of the paper as long as he got the sports section, neat and ready to read.

Up in my room again, I took my typewriter off the desk and set it on the floor. I pushed the vase I kept pens and pencils in to the side of the desk and opened the paper to the want ads.

I grabbed a felt-tipped pen, uncapped it, had it ready.

There were a lot of prospects, just like in Sunday's paper, that is, if you know all about computers, which I don't. I read every square inch of the help wanted ads, but I didn't see anything I could use. And I meant I'd take anything as long as I didn't have to go near a stove or food.

I guess Mama could've used her influence to get me a job at the hospital, but I couldn't see me serving food for four hours a night. I simply did not want to serve food, or even work around it. Cook it, either. So I looked over the ads again, making sure I hadn't missed anything. I hadn't.

From out in the hallway, Mama said, "Miranda, you got the paper?"

"Yes, I have it."

"Give me a section."

I got up and went to the door. I gave her a

section. There really wasn't anything else in it that interested me. Although I'd marked a job that I could check out after school. I clipped out the ad and taped it to my binder so I could have it handy. I even thought some about cutting school, but I couldn't blot my perfect attendance record. That'd look good on a job application.

'Out in the hallway, Mama said, "What have you done? You've got ink all over the paper."

"I had to mark the jobs that were interesting, didn't I?"

My room door was ajar. She pushed it all the way open and came in. "You know you could start out doing some baby-sitting. There's always a need for that." She didn't wait for me to answer. Trying not to get ink on her hands, she folded the paper and went downstairs.

Baby-sitting wasn't a bad idea, I thought. Besides, I had experience doing that. Of course, it'd probably take a thousand baby-sitting jobs to earn enough to get contact lenses. I looked at my watch. It was almost four-thirty. I got up and went downstairs.

"Where are you going?" Mama asked when she saw me heading for the front door.

"To the corner grocery. To the laundromat. I'm gonna put ads on their bulletin boards."

All Mama said was, "Be careful."

A week later, I got a call from one of the ads. I'd already baby-sat for Mr. and Mrs. Taliaferro when I was thirteen. I almost did cartwheels all the way downstairs when I went to tell Mama what'd happened.

When I got through telling Mama about it, I knew I had to get upstairs and start back to reading that novel. I ran upstairs almost as swiftly as I'd come down them.

In my room, I was so excited I didn't want to concentrate enough to read. But I knew I had to. Over the weeks, I had read a lot, but I was still far from finished, although I could see the end of the book. I had one hundred and eighty-odd pages to go. In order to save time, instead of typing a paper, I decided to give an oral book report. I also realized I'd have to slow down some if I were to remember anything that was on those pages. In order to help me slow down, I got a pen and a five-by-eight pad and jotted notes for my book report.

Right in the middle of my note taking, I thought about what I was doing, what I'd thought earlier. *I* was going to give an oral report? Me? Although Mrs. DeRoy hadn't said anything, I was the only one in the class who hadn't given an oral report. Some kids had given them twice.

Maybe it'd help me get a job. I'd have to talk to everybody in order to get a job.

Every once in a while, while I was reading, I thought about the money I'd earn baby-sitting for people. If they told their friends, I'd soon have a lot of money, I thought. I couldn't wait.

But first, I had to give my book report. I hoped Mrs. DeRoy would invite Mrs. Storm to sit in on the class when I gave my book report. She often did that with other teachers who had a free period. I would cut Mrs. Storm's favorite author to pieces. That'd make things perfect.

So many good things were happening. I had a baby-sitting job all lined up. With a little luck, it'd lead to others. I was finishing the book I wanted to read for my book report, I had a job lead to check out, and Teena and I were going job hunting on Tuesday.

I stopped reading and sprawled across my bed on my stomach, indulging myself in my contact lens fantasy. Now, I thought, meet the new Miranda L. Moses. My thick glasses slid down my nose. I didn't care. I just pushed them up again.

If things kept looking up, it was going to be a great summer, a rich summer.

SEVEN

On Friday afternoon, Mrs. DeRoy seemed delighted that I was finally giving an oral book report. But I had picked the worst day for it, because it rained, and rain drummed on the roof all day long. Since my English class is on the top floor, we could hear the rain louder than other classes did. I guess.

Anyway, Mrs. DeRoy said, "Class, we have a treat. Miranda will give a report on one of our more popular novelists." To me, she said, "Now, you really project so you can be heard over the rain and all the way in the back of the room."

I mumbled softly, "All right." Mrs. DeRoy got a notepad and a pen and moved to one of the vacant desks in the back of the room. She sat in a corner right below the windows.

The lectern up near Mrs. DeRoy's desk was

only about four feet from my desk. It seemed like ten miles from where I stood. On legs about as strong as a salad mold made of Jell-O, I made my way up to the lectern.

I sat on a high stool that was there and placed my notes and the big novel on the lectern. The stool was a bit rickety and squeaked when I sat down. I stared out at the sea of faces that belonged to my classmates.

They stared back, waiting.

With the class staring at me like that, there wasn't anything I could do except begin. So I did.

I gave the title of the book and the author's name. "This writer," I said, "has a wonderful sense of place. If I ever go to Arizona, where the story is set, I feel pretty sure I'll have no trouble finding this little town."

I pushed my glasses up, then continued: "Only thing wrong, I feel he was a little too cruel to his characters. I realize a writer has to be cruel to his characters so you can care about them. His characters weren't nothing but paper dolls. The same kind I used to play with when I was a little kid." I was quiet until they stopped laughing, then I gave a synopsis of the story. Afterwards, I asked if there were any questions. A few hands went up.

Pointing to the back of the room, I called on Craig. He was sitting in front of Mrs. DeRoy. Craig stood and cleared his throat. He was lots taller and skinnier than I remembered. He said, "Would you read another one of this writer's books?"

"Only if it's thinner."

The class laughed again. Craig bent his lanky legs and sank back into his seat.

I said, "I don't think he needed to give me all the information he gave for me to enjoy the story." I glanced back at Mrs. DeRoy. She was nodding slowly.

Mrs. DeRoy said, "Miranda, don't you think the fact that the scenery is so well defined is because of the characters? They're pretty sharply drawn, I thought."

"I've never thought of it in that way, but I don't think they were as big as their surroundings. I can't remember their names without consulting my notes. Looks like I should be able to remember at least one character if they were well drawn."

"Okay," Mrs. DeRoy said.

"Readers today watch TV. They know a lot of things. They probably know how a small town looks. I think he should've used some of the detail for his characters."

I wished Mrs. Storm could've come. I wanted to know what she thought. Anyway, I was glad Mrs. DeRoy had let us choose what we wanted to read.

"Are there any more questions?" I asked. I

looked around the room, thinking: This is fun. I didn't want to leave. I was disappointed when nobody asked any more questions. I could've stayed there another half hour. And nobody had booed or hissed, either.

I slipped off the squeaky stool and got my notes and my book off the lectern and went back to my seat. As I sat down, I gave a sigh of relief. Maybe I'd get a bonus grade. I kind of wished it was earlier in the semester so I could give another oral book report. My nervousness had disappeared ten seconds after I'd given the class the title of the book.

There were only a few minutes before the bell would ring. Outside, it was still raining. It pounded on the roof, and sheets of rain splattered the windowpanes. I gathered up my things, getting ready to go home. Before I'd finished stacking my books neatly, the bell rang. Kids scrambled out of their seats and into the hallway.

I lifted my books into my left arm.

Mrs. DeRoy had already gone back to her desk. As I was about to walk past, she said, "Miranda, could you wait a second —"

I edged my way over to her desk. She said, "That was a wonderful book report. I don't see why you were so afraid of standing up in front of the class. It's a pity you didn't do it sooner. That way, we could look forward to getting a treat from you several times a year. I'm giving you an A."

"Thanks," I said, sheepishly.

"Don't thank me. You earned it." She smiled at me and started stacking the books and papers on her desk.

" 'Bye," I said as I started for the door.

"Keep reading," Mrs. DeRoy said.

"I will," I assured her and went out of the classroom.

I went down to my locker. I hoped that there was a raincoat in there that I'd forgotten to take home. Or at least an old ragged umbrella. My locker was chock-full of so much stuff, no telling what was in there. I couldn't keep it as neat as I did my closet at home. But then, Mama didn't come around inspecting my locker the way she did my closet.

When I'd opened my locker, I saw that there wasn't a raincoat in it. I started cramming my books into Daddy's old leather briefcase, when I spied a ragged purple umbrella way in the back. I pushed aside some books and a small mayonnaise jar of pennies and took the umbrella out. A piece of it fell off on the locker shelf. The umbrella was automatic. I pressed the doohickey to see if it'd open. It did. At least, most of it did. I saw that the thing that'd fallen was off the umbrella onto the shelf was a folded metal rib. I closed the umbrella, tucked it under my arm, grabbed the briefcase, and slammed my locker door shut.

By the time I got to the first floor, I knew the ragged old umbrella wouldn't do a bit of good in the rain that was falling. I had no other choice but to try to use it. Looked like somebody'd already used it for a club. I'd probably swatted the Shephards' Great Dane with it. Maybe that's why he was always chasing me.

On the front steps of the school, I popped open the umbrella and looked up through the big hole in it, then walked on to the bus stop.

While I waited for the bus, I hoped that getting a summer job would be halfway as easy as standing up in front of my classmates and giving an oral book report. But somehow I knew it wouldn't.

EIGHT

On Monday, I stopped at the pet store and almost put in an application. I had to pick up some food for my two goldfish. Working in a pet store wouldn't've been so bad. I'd do anything, even clean the animals' cages. But something in little see-through cases stopped me from applying. The little cases looked like small aquariums. A whole stack of them near the counter had the biggest and hairiest tarantulas I'd ever seen. I paid for the fish food and backed out of the store.

Maybe I'd have better luck on Tuesday when Teena and I went hunting for a job for me, I thought. I did so want to get a job before school closed. I thought I stood a much better chance if I did. All the kids wouldn't be out looking. There was still a half a week to go.

On Tuesday when Teena and I got back from town, Mama was home. I thought she'd gone to work, but she'd simply slept in since she'd taken a personal day.

She worked me pretty near to death. We washed the woodwork in the kitchen. When that was done, she hinted very strongly that my room could use a thorough cleaning. I thought my room looked pretty nice except for a thousand of Teena's CDs strewn all over one side of it. But I did go and give my room the once-over. Actually, I really did a nice job of cleaning it. For a change. If you've ever tried to clean dustballs off carpets from underneath a bed, then you know what a job that is.

Only thing I didn't do, I didn't stack the CDs. They were still scattered all over the chest of drawers. There was a great pile of CDs on the floor on both sides of the chest of drawers, too. I was saving them for Teena, see if I could get her to pick them up and take them home. I was going to have a talk with her about them someday soon.

I went and sprawled across my bed, resting up. Mama yelled upstairs, "Miranda, we've got to finish the woodwork in the dining room."

Naturally, I thought the dining room woodwork only needed a good wiping with a dry cloth, but Mama had other ideas. I heard her in the kitchen running water. Pretty soon, the scent of some kind of pine cleanser wafted its way upstairs. I eased off the bed. "I'm coming," I said. I hoped she could tell by my voice that I was too tired to do much of anything.

Mama and I got the woodwork done. Then, she went and took a shower and slipped on a pair of khaki slacks, like work pants, and a red blouse. She went into the living room and slid into the big blue corduroy chair by the window. She picked up the suspense thriller she'd been reading before washing walls had interrupted her.

I went into the living room and slumped onto the sofa. "Mama," I said. I leaned back, my head resting against the back of the sofa. I wanted to take a shower, too, but I was too tired.

"Yes — " Mama glanced up from her book. Her eyes looked extra large through the lenses of her round eyeglasses — of course, not as big as my own.

"How can I cook supper every other night or so if I'm going to also have a job?"

Mama closed her book on a slender brown finger so she wouldn't lose her place. She gazed at me, smiling slyly. "I've been doing it for years," she said. "It's difficult but not impossible."

"But in September, I'll have homework, too. And, I hope, a job."

"I know."

"I might not be able to cook until late."

"You can do homework while you cook."

"I've tried that. I burned my arm. I burned a whole pot of rice," I said. I looked at my arm. There was no sign I'd been burned. "The pot was burned to a crisp."

"Miranda, honey, you'll work something out. Believe me, I wouldn't have you do this, but it's important. You'll thank me one of these days."

Yeah, sure, right, I thought, but didn't dare say it.

Before she opened her book again, she added, "Fix something delicious and interesting for dinner."

"Good grief! Is it my turn again already?"

Mama smiled and opened her book. I kind of hoped she'd call out for a pizza. I'm sure she had eight dollars tucked away somewhere.

I pulled myself up off the sofa and went and threw out the scrub water and put the bucket under the sink. When I went back through the living room, headed upstairs to shower, Mama was lost in her suspense thriller.

After my shower, I made beans and wieners and sauerkraut for dinner. I don't know if it was interesting, but anybody can make that, and it would've tasted better if someone else had cooked.

I had timed the meal perfectly. By the time Mama and Daddy and I had eaten, it was time to go across the street and up the block to stay with Kenny and Kirk, the Taliaferro twins.

NINE

Although it had been a year or more since I'd been to the Taliaferro house, I'd forgotten how big it was. Their house was in the same neighborhood as mine, but it was older and lots bigger. There were two picture windows in the front of the house on either side of the door. It looked like some huge monster, painted a pale green with a dark brown door that looked like a mouth and nose made into one. A sooty brick chimney poked up over the black shingles of the roof.

Inside, they had an attic and a large basement. Where my house had three bedrooms, theirs had four and a half. I guess they planned to separate Kenny and Kirk when they got older.

And they had a big yard, front and back, so the twins could have plenty of room. The lawn looked like spanking brand-new velvet, not a brown patch on it anywhere.

Kirk and Kenny must've been watching out of one of the windows for me. I stood on their stoop, reaching to ring the doorbell, when the door swung open. The twins stood there grinning at me.

The twins were six or seven, at least. They were the most active kids in the world. I think one of them might've been a little less active than the other, but not much. I stood on the threshold and stared. I couldn't tell them apart.

I stepped inside the wide foyer, and one of the twins closed the door behind me and locked it. Over to the left was the living room. An ebony baby grand piano stood near the picture window. There was a fireplace with a shining glass screen. But the one thing that held my attention the most was out in the foyer.

A new large aquarium stood against the cream-colored wall. It was on an iron stand. Greenish light gleamed eerily from the aquarium. I saw fish in every color of the rainbow. The only ones that I recognized were the Jack Dempsey and the sun-fish and the baby shark. The sunfish looked vaguely like my goldfish. It was bigger than the rest of them, including the shark. It went swim-ming around the tank, slapping the smaller fish with its tail. Its bright orange color made it stand out like a brand-new penny sparkling in the sun.

"You got an aquarium?" one of the twins asked.

"No. Just a couple of goldfish. This is really nice," I said, peering into the tank.

"Kirk gave all the fish names," Kenny said, pointing to his brother.

"No, I didn't," Kirk said, and gave his brother a push.

Kenny grabbed Kirk, and they started shoving each other and tussling until they bumped into the aquarium. Water sloshed; the fish trembled and swam away from the front of the tank.

Just then, Mr. and Mrs. Taliaferro came into the foyer, dressed to go out.

Mrs. Taliaferro frowned and shouted, "Boys! Boys! Now, none of that!"

That didn't stop them. They kept on going at each other. Then, Mr. Taliaferro cleared his throat, and when they stopped for a second, he gave them a look. He kind of lowered his head and frowned at them. Right away, they moved into the living room and sat on the great blue sofa and, using the remote control unit, turned on the TV. They sat there watching it.

"Hello, Miranda, how are you?" Mrs. Taliaferro said to me.

Almost before I could say, "Fine," Mrs. Taliaferro opened her little purse and took out a pair of dark-framed eyeglasses. They reminded me of my glasses, but the lenses weren't thick at all. Self-consciously, I reached and pushed my own glasses up, although they didn't need it.

Mrs. Taliaferro put on her glasses and started giving me a thousand and one instructions on what to do if there's an emergency. " — and eat anything you want. The boys can have milk and cookies. Popcorn is okay, too. No pop under any circumstances."

She took up the pad by the telephone and looked at it a long time, frowning all the while. She turned the pad over and I saw it'd been written on. "This is where we'll be." She pushed up her glasses. "I hope you can get through if you need us. I'll bet they don't even have Call-Waiting."

All this time, Mr. Taliaferro was looking at his watch. He didn't say a word. Then he opened the door and said, "Miranda's kept the boys before."

"I know. That was nearly two years ago."

Mrs. Taliaferro pulled off her glasses, tucked them back into a case, and put the case back into her purse. She looked around as if wondering if she'd forgotten something.

"Woman, we're going to be late," Mr. Taliaferro said, and grabbed his wife's arm. She dropped the pad she'd been holding. I went and picked it up. I looked at it and saw she'd even written my own phone number amid the numbers I was to call in an emergency.

Still holding his wife's hand, Mr. Taliaferro started for the door. Mrs. Taliaferro looked back and yelled, "And you can call your mother — "

I didn't hear the rest of it. Mr. Taliaferro had pulled his wife out of the house.

After they'd gone, the house was strangely quiet. The only sound was the gurgle and hum of the aquarium.

I went and bolted the door. I didn't need to leave it open since they had the air conditioner going.

"Draw the curtains," one of the twins said. Sunlight streamed in, making it hard to see the TV screen.

I went around behind the baby grand piano and pulled the curtains closed. They were very thick curtains and made the room dark.

Going back to the sofa, I sat down. I didn't want to be in a house that big in the dark, so I reached over and flicked on one of the lamps.

What are we going to do for entertainment? I thought as I glanced at the twins. That's one good thing about baby-sitting. Sometimes it's as much entertainment as it is work.

TEN

In the few minutes it'd taken their parents to get into the car and drive off, the twins had gotten tired of playing with the TV remote control. One of them put it gently on the lamp table. They sat side by side on the sofa.

Although I'd seen them do almost everything together, one of them got up and went through the dining room and out to the kitchen.

Shortly, the twin came back. "Miranda, it's getting dark outdoors. Can we play ball in the house?"

"Don't break anything. Use a plastic ball," I said. I was pretty sure they had one because I'd noticed a plastic bat leaning across the pedestal base of the dining room table.

The twins ran upstairs, their footsteps muffled on the thick stairway carpet. They came back down with an official regulation-sized baseball. I leapt up and headed across the room to take it away from them.

Since they were across the room from me and a little more — no, a lot more — sprightly than I was, I didn't make it. I'd always thought I was tall, my legs long, but I guess that wasn't the case. Before I could step around the huge oval coffee table, and get midway across the room, one of the twins drew back and threw the ball. I felt cool air as it whizzed past my head.

Then I heard a crack. A sound like you should hear only in the ballpark. The sound you would've heard if a batter had hit a home run.

But we weren't in a ball park. We were in the Taliaferros' living room.

I turned. I didn't want to do it. I didn't want to face what I had to face. And then I heard glass falling and breaking. And water splashing down like in a waterfall. Like a real heavy rain had broken a dam somewhere.

As far as I got was the edge of the carpets in the living room. Water gushed out of the aquarium. That huge tank in the foyer looked like a creek after a flood. The baseball was still in the tank. I don't know why I noticed that. I guess because most of the fish were flip-flopping on the hardwood floor.

Water was everywhere. It hadn't quite oozed onto the carpet, but it was going to if I didn't mop it up. And soon. I couldn't seem to decide what to do first. Should I pick up the broken glass? Should I put the fish into another container? What? What? I think it was the sight of the poor homeless fish that made me do something. Some of them looked like they were already dead. Others flopped around on the polished hardwood floor, gasping for air, their eyes closed, their mouths opening and closing like mad.

I started to pick up the glass, then I saw that I needed something to put it in. I glanced at the twins out of the corner of my eye. They were staring at the fish. When they saw me looking, they started pointing to each other.

"One of you go get me a mop."

Before they moved, there was an argument about who would bring the mop.

"Go get the mop," I said again, more firmly.

While they were getting the mop, I dashed into the kitchen to see if there was something big enough to put the fish in.

I threw open cupboard doors. All I saw were willow blue dishes everywhere, none of them big enough to hold the fish. I looked in the cabinets under the sink. I almost gave up and was going to put them in the bathtub until I spied a big cabinet door next to the dishwasher. I yanked it open.

Kneeling down, I saw there was the biggest punch bowl in the world. I eased it out of the cabinet. There was a medium-sized punch bowl inside it. I got them both and set them on the counter next to the sink. I kicked the cabinet door closed with my foot. The two bowls clinked together as I carried them back into the living room.

As I bent to pick up the fish, I suddenly thought about the twins. They were taking too long to get the mop. I hoped they weren't getting into more trouble.

More of the fish had stopped moving, had stopped gasping for air. I picked up the ones I knew were still alive and put them into the punch bowls. It was rough going since they were so slippery, but I got them all into the bowls and carried them into the kitchen. I set the bowls on the counter near the sink and got a pitcher and started filling the bowls with cold water. When they were filled, I pushed the bowls farther back on the counter, hopefully out of Kirk and Kenny's reach. Since I'd used both bowls, the fish had room to swim. They swam around and around. I stood back and admired my handiwork. The punch bowls made pretty good aquariums.

The twins finally came back with the mop. I took it and mopped the water that was still oozing toward the carpet. Kenny and Kirk stepped in the water and made footprints on the dry part of the floor.

"Stop that!" I yelled. "Go watch TV!"

They didn't move toward the TV, but they did

stop making tracks. I stopped mopping and looked at them, my arms akimbo. They both flashed me the sweetest smiles, then ran upstairs.

From the top of the stairs, they both said, "We'll watch TV up here."

After a while, I heard the TV. I went into the kitchen and got a box to pick up the glass.

When the glass was picked up, I put old newspapers in the wet spot to finish absorbing the water. Earlier, I'd seen the papers stacked on the floor in the walk-in pantry, right next to one of those thingamajigs that's used to roll newspapers into logs for the fireplace.

After the papers were soaked, I picked them up, hoping I wouldn't get a sliver of glass into a finger. I'm glad I didn't. I dumped the soggy paper into the kitchen garbage can. Using the mop again, I dried the floor as best I could. Then I took the mop back to the back porch.

Coming in again, I made sure the back door was locked and I joined the twins upstairs.

Before I could go into their parents' bedroom, where they were watching TV, I could hear the eerie music. I pushed the door open. It creaked as if the hinges were crusty with rust. I stood in the doorway, my eyes fixed on the TV screen. What I saw wasn't the kind of movie little boys ought to watch. And on the screen, when a big hairy hand wielding a butcher knife lashed out at someone, I knew it wasn't the kind of movie a teenage girl alone with two little boys ought to watch, either.

"Change the channel!" I screamed, still standing in the doorway.

"Ah, Miranda," they said in unison, but one of them did get up and change the channel.

"If there's a remote control, give it here," I said.

"This is our old TV. It don't have a remote," one of them said.

He flicked the dial until he found an old movie in black and white. I went on into the room and watched TV for a while. The three of us sat in an oversized chair and watched TV. The chair had a bright green crushed velvet slipcover. The whole Taliaferro master bedroom was done up in shades of green and red. It looked like it was decorated for Christmas.

I hadn't realized how tired I was until I sank onto the cushiony soft chair. I could've stayed there until the Taliaferros came home. I certainly hoped the twins would sit in the chair with me until they got sleepy, but I knew they wouldn't.

"I want a cookie," one twin said.

"And pop," his brother added.

Naturally, they'd want what they couldn't have. Everybody does.

"Put on your pajamas first," I said.

"My mother lets us stay up till twelve o'clock," one twin said.

"Let's get one thing straight," I said. "I'm not your mother."

Together, they said, "Ah, Miranda — "

"Put on your pajamas," I said, sharply. They went off and put on their pajamas. At least, one of them came back.

"Where's your brother?"

I was scared to ask which twin he was. I wished I knew how to tell them apart. The twin dressed in baby blue pajamas climbed into the chair beside me. He was clutching a picture book.

With big brown eyes, he looked up at me and smiled. I gave him a wan smile back. "I'm Kirk," he said. "Read this." He handed me the book.

"Where's Kenny?"

He shrugged, then sniffed the air. "He must be making popcorn. I think I smell it. Don't you smell something?"

I sniffed and pushed Kirk and his picture book aside. I leapt out of the chair. Although I'd sniffed, I didn't smell anything. But, halfway downstairs, I got the scent of hot buttered popcorn. By then, I could also hear the automatic corn popper. I don't know what I would've done if he'd burned himself or broken something else.

But by the time I got to the kitchen, Kenny was safe and sound. He'd finished popping corn and had already unplugged the corn popper and was pouring the popped corn into a large paper grocery bag. He looked at me as I came into the kitchen.

"Mama says I can soak up some of the butter-oil if I put it into a bag like this," Kenny said. "We always make popcorn when we sit up watching TV."

I was so relieved that nothing had been broken and that Kenny hadn't been broken that I just leaned against the kitchen doorjamb and rubbed my arm over my face and head. They were getting on my last nerve. I couldn't wait for next week so I could go looking for a real job again.

Kenny set the bag of popcorn on the kitchen table and pushed a chair over to the cupboard.

"What're you doing now?" I asked.

He didn't answer. He climbed up on the chair, opened a cupboard door, and took down a small willow blue bowl. He got off the chair and pushed it back to the table. He dipped the bowl into the bag and scooped it full of popped corn. He handed it to me.

"Have some," he said, and smiled.

I took the bowl. I started feeling guilty for thinking the twins were getting on my nerves. I grabbed a fistful of popcorn and ate it. It was delicious, melted in my mouth. Food is always good when somebody else do the cooking. Even if it's a seven-year-old boy.

Carrying the bag of popcorn, Kenny went out of the kitchen. When we were in the dining room,

Kenny stopped and said, "You know how Mama and Daddy tell us apart?"

You mean it can be done? I thought. I said, "How?"

"Kirk has a scar at the front of his head. It's more like a dent. It's always been there. You probably just didn't pay much attention to him. Most grown-ups think we just look like two peas in a pod. When we get upstairs, look at the right side of his forehead, just where his hair stops."

"Okay," I said.

"Miranda," Kenny said, "don't let him see you looking. He don't like for anybody to know he got a dent." Kenny laughed.

I laughed, too, and Kenny and I went upstairs.

Up in their parents' bedroom, there was a TV tray. He slid it closer to the green chair and set the bag of popcorn on it. He and Kirk started eating. I eased back into the chair next to Kirk, all the time staring at his forehead. At first I didn't see it, but then I looked even closer, and there it was. A little dent.

I got the picture book off the bedside table and read it to them. The TV blared in the background, but both of them sat quietly beside me and listened.

At nine o'clock, they went to bed. I didn't really have to coax them. By the time the story was over, they were getting drowsy. I tucked them in, then went back to their parents' bedroom and turned off the TV, so it wouldn't waken them.

With the twins asleep, I got a little skittish. The house was too quiet with the TV off. The house started creaking and popping, settling for the night. I don't know why houses do that. All I know is that all I thought about was the movie I'd made the twins turn away from. I kept seeing that big hairy hand lashing out with the knife.

I started to stay in the room with the twins, but that was just too much. Besides, their chairs were little bitty things, made just for kids. I could sit in them all right, but I had a feeling I'd get stuck in one, or break it, like Goldilocks. So I got the rest of the popcorn and went downstairs. I turned on the new TV, as the twins called it, and found an old movie comedy from the fifties. Nobody had told me I couldn't have pop at night, so I went and got a can of Dr Pepper out of the fridge, then went back to the living room and settled down and watched the movie.

When the Taliaferros returned, I was sitting in the living room, sipping Dr Pepper and watching the movie.

"What happened here?" Mr. Taliaferro exclaimed as he surveyed the ruined aquarium. I hadn't taken the baseball out of the tank. At least I'd remembered to unplug the aquarium light.

"There was an accident," I explained lamely.

"Otherwise, everything's all right?" Mrs. Taliaferro asked.

"Yes."

They looked at what was left of the aquarium again. "I should've known." She didn't seem mad at all. "This'll come out of their allowances."

"Come on, Miranda," Mr. Taliaferro said, "I'll take you home."

"I'm sorry about the aquarium," I said when we were outside. We walked the few blocks to my house.

"Don't worry about it, Miranda," Mr. Taliaferro said. "It just needs another sheet of glass."

Mr. Taliaferro waited on the stoop at my house until I'd unlocked the door and gone inside.

Up in my room, I put the money I'd earned into the vase where I kept pens and pencils, then got undressed and got into bed.

ELEVEN

On Wednesday of the next week, I still hadn't found a real job. When I was getting dressed for school — there were four days left — I thought about skipping them and just spending the days placing applications, but I didn't.

Aside from the fact that Mama would've had a conniption fit if she found out, I was concerned about how it'd look on my record. After all, I did want to go to college.

So I went to school.

At the end of the week, I had to pick up a few things for Mama at the supermarket. It seemed like she had not only delegated some of the cooking to me, but a lot of the shopping, too. I was going to the store with amazing regularity lately. Ordinarily, she would've gone to the store herself, just to look at the books. The supermarket,

Produceland, had a whole bookstore inside.

At Produceland I checked the bulletin board. Of course there wasn't anything interesting on it. I was about to turn away and go do my shopping when a big poster on the wall to the left of the bulletin board caught my eye. I read it carefully, twice, then fished a felt-tipped pen out of my purse. I jotted the highlights from the poster on a scrap of paper I'd found in my purse. What I really wanted to do was rip the whole poster off the wall and roll it up and tuck it under my arm and take it with me. I wondered how long it had been there. But that didn't matter much now.

I was so excited, I could hardly finish my shopping. My heart thumped like it was gonna bust loose out of my chest. I kept smiling to myself. I couldn't stop no matter how hard I tried. Other shoppers were looking at me like I'd lost my last marble, but I didn't care. I knew I'd finally found something good.

By the time I got on the bus with my groceries, I realized I hadn't really needed to copy so much information off the poster. I had that thing memorized. I went over it again and again in my head as I rode the bus home. The words from the poster screamed in my head:

JUNIOR COUNSELORS * 16 AND OLDER
SPEND THE NEXT TWO WEEKS WITH US

And there was a phone number to call. I knew it by heart, too. Everything on the poster interested me, but I didn't really need any exercise. I got more than I wanted dodging and ducking the Shephards' Great Dane.

When the bus drew up to my stop, I hefted the bag up in one arm. I had taken the scrap of paper out of my purse. I clutched it tight. As tight as if it had been a hundred-dollar bill. To me, it was as valuable as that. Even more. Like if I worked the whole two weeks I'd earn a small fortune.

I thought about the age. I wasn't sixteen, but I would be in a little over a year. One year wouldn't matter. I pushed the thought aside. Sixteen was just a technicality.

I was so excited and keyed up, I forgot to watch out for the Great Dane. I was going up the front walk when I spied the great elephant of a dog. He was sprawled under the big maple tree on the Shephards' front lawn, cooling off, I guess. The day was so hot, you could've scrambled eggs on the sidewalk. I started walking faster and turned onto the walkway to my house.

The Great Dane turned his head in my direction but didn't get up. He soon turned back to look in the next yard, where a couple of kids were taking a shower, running under their sprinkler.

The dog was more interested in them than in me right then.

Still glancing at the dog, I made it all the way up on the stoop. I got the door opened before I heard the dog growl low behind me. He sounded hot, tired, hungry, and angry. Although I nearly dropped the bag of groceries, I pulled the door open and dashed inside. The Great Dane ran up on the stoop, huffing and puffing, and looked in through the screen at me. I hooked the screen door.

"Missed me that time, boy," I said. I went and put the groceries on the table. I didn't bother about putting them away right then. Never mind that I might've bought something that was perishable. I couldn't even remember what I'd bought. I just grabbed the kitchen phone and started dialing.

While I waited for an answer, I pulled a chair out from the table and sat down. From where I sat, I could still keep my eye on the Great Dane. He was still sitting on the stoop, his tongue lolling out, panting. I don't know why he was out to get me. I mean, he and I are neighbors. What bad thing did I ever do to him?

The phone rang and rang in my ear. I hung up and redialed, making sure I hadn't dialed the wrong number.

Outside, the Great Dane pressed his horsey head against the screen door, peering into the house. The only thing I can remember is that once I'd given him a plastic dog bone I'd found on the bus. It had been spanking brand-new. I'd tried to turn it in to the bus driver, but he'd said, "Kid, the lost and found department got enough stuff down there. Must be two, three million items down there. You got a dog, give it to him."

So I'd given the plastic dog bone to the Shephards' Great Dane. I just unwrapped it and pitched it across the fence into their backyard.

All that had happened about a month or so after we moved next door to the Shephards. The bone was pretty chewed up now, but the dog still played with it.

In my ear, a woman's voice said, "Hello," and I forgot all about the Great Dane.

"My name is Miranda L. Moses," I said. "I'm calling about one of your poster ads — "

Fifteen minutes later when I'd hung up, I was registered as a junior camp counselor.

TWELVE

That night at supper, I told Mama and Daddy what I'd done. I had to because I needed a note of permission. The eighteen-year-old kids didn't. I wished I'd said I was eighteen.

It was Mama's day to cook. She'd fried chicken and made potato salad, and broccoli, my favorite vegetable. We were eating in the dining room. She'd said you don't eat a meal like that in the kitchen. We had the air-conditioning blasting on account of it was so hot that night. Mama had brought along a quart of vanilla ice cream for dessert. So she wouldn't have to make anything, I guess. I thought that was cheating. When it was my turn to cook, she'd let me serve ice cream only once. She always made me make dessert from scratch, even if it was only chocolate pudding.

Later, when Mama and I did the dishes, I said, "Just think. A real grown-up job."

"How much you say it pays?" my father asked from the living room, where he'd gone to read the sports page. Mama wouldn't let him read it at the dining room table. She'd said, "Mike, it's okay in the morning, but not at suppertime."

I told him how much I'd earn and went right back to wiping plates.

Mama said, "Miranda, I don't want you going so far away."

"It's just thirty miles or so," I told her as I dried another dish and put it into the cupboard.

"I don't care," Mama said, her hands deep in the hot sudsy water. "You're too young to go traipsing off so far."

Sometimes fathers get in your corner. Daddy said from the living room, "Justine, she's bound to go away to college one of these days."

Mama pursed her lips and didn't say another word all the while we washed dishes. As soon as we'd finished, she wiped her hands on her apron, untied it, tossed it across the back of a chair, and went to the desk in the living room, where she scribbled me a permission slip. Handing it to me, she said, "All right, Miranda, I still have misgivings about all of this."

I grinned and took the note and folded it and went upstairs and tucked it into the inside pocket of my purse.

On Saturday, a week later, my parents juggled their schedules and drove me downtown to catch the bus that'd take me to the camp. They didn't wait, didn't see me off. Anyway, I felt a little like I was already going off to college. I almost cried when I saw their car drive away and disappear in the midst of the Saturday traffic.

There were other kids there. Some real little kids going off to camp for the first time who clung to their parents, and others like me who were going to get paid for being camp counselors. I scrutinized them. All the bigger kids looked like they were sixteen years old. Some even looked eighteen and might've been. That made my fourteen and a half seem as young as a fourteen-month-old baby. I look back sometimes and realize I got away with this because I'm tall and gangly. Not as tall and gangly as Catriona Maryland, but tall and gangly just the same.

I waited with the other camp counselors under the city bus shelter, just as I'd been instructed. They were going to pick us up at eleven o'clock. I looked at my watch. It was five to eleven. I looked at the other counselors again. There was baggage all over the sidewalk. I'd probably brought more clothes than I would need. I had two bags. Big bags. I'd packed all the shorts and lightweight summer clothes I owned. Mama had said, "You'd better take some warm clothing. It's going to get cold in the woods. You know how you shiver in the least little breeze."

Reluctantly, I'd packed a few pair of pants, too. But no jeans. I thought they'd be too hot. Thank goodness I'd packed a hooded cardigan-style sweatshirt.

At eleven o'clock, a big white school bus drew up to the curb. On the side of the bus was written in large letters, CAMP MUCKALUCK. Someone had drawn a pair of wrinkled old boots below the camp name.

They opened the rear doors and we loaded our stuff, then climbed on. We were off.

I was a little nervous as I sat in a window seat watching the scenery change from city to rural. Some of the others seemed to be as nervous as I was. They sat looking out the windows, too. Only a few talked a lot. They chattered on and on as the bus sped along the highway past thick woods, then over a trestle on a river so bright I had to close my eyes. Not look at it at all.

Then through farmland, crops thriving in fields as far as the eye could see.

At long last, a clearing. About a hundred yards from the highway stood the camp, an old log cabin that might've been left over from a couple of centuries ago.

The bus pulled off the paved road and onto a rocky dirt road and inched its way to the front of the log cabin. The bus creaked to a stop. We sat there dazed. Or just plain tired. I was tired from the long ride, and I guess they were, too. I know I've never had to sit in one place for almost an hour without getting up and doing something else. Or going somewhere else, either.

Maybe it was the appearance of the cabin. It looked like Abraham Lincoln would've been around back splitting rails or something. I don't know what I really expected. But I did know this wasn't it.

I got my bags — slung them both over my weary shoulders — and got off the bus.

Standing on the gravel walkway, I wondered what I had gotten myself into.

THIRTEEN

I stood on the porch of the log cabin that was the office of the camp and filled my lungs with warm, clean air. Actually, the log cabin wasn't a bad-looking building. It had a rustic air, I guess because it was made of logs, with a larger cabin for campers. Tall pines stood around the cabin that we would live in. I wondered if it was too late to change my mind.

The early June sun boiled down to let me know that the dog days soon to come would make things as hot as the Sahara Desert. It wasn't cooler at camp at all. I think it might've been a hundred degrees in the shade. I could look along the horizon and see heat rays shimmering.

From not too far off, a creek cut through the woods. I could see parts of it like a gigantic silver ribbon gleaming in the noonday sun. It sparkled so, I couldn't look at it straight on. It was just as hard to look at as the river we'd crossed earlier.

Even on that first afternoon, I missed Mama and Daddy and Teena, with her endless CD collection. After the first three or four days, I even started to miss Catriona Maryland. That's just how desperate I was to get home, back to civilization. I didn't expect camp to be so — so countrified.

All that came later. But first, I had to take care of five little girls they assigned to me. As their group leader, I had to make sure they were happy and content, make sure they didn't get lost.

I got the girls lined up early and stood out in front of the cabin waiting for the others to join us. I stood there in the shade of a pine tree, sizing up the girls, trying to remember their names. There was Octavia, a tall, thin girl who came up to my shoulder. I couldn't believe she was only seven. She had two long braids hanging down her back and wore glasses with lenses almost as thick as my own. Next to her was a short girl with tiny freckles dotting her moon face. I couldn't think of her name.

She stepped away from the group and said, "Miranda, are there bears 'round here? My brother says there is. He's twelve and reads a lotta books. He says bears always live in woods like this." She looked around. She was probably only about six years old.

91

"Nonsense," I said, hoping my voice didn't sound too shaky. I felt shaky. My voice sounded shaky to me. "I don't think there're any bears around here." I hoped I was more convincing than I felt. " — Er, what's your name again?"

Moving closer to me, her arms behind her back, she said, simply, "Edda."

"Edda, don't you worry about a thing." Miranda's on the job, I thought.

"Miranda," Octavia said, "I think I hear a bear rustling through that grass." She pushed up her glasses, then pointed over my shoulder. I turned and tried to peer deeper into the woods.

In the direction Octavia had pointed, the grass was moving, like a strong wind was blowing through it. There was a crunch and a snap as if someone had stepped on a twig. I didn't see anything, especially a bear. I didn't want to see anything, especially a bear. All I saw was the narrow creek stretching endlessly and sparkling like someone was holding a mirror up to the sun. I listened closer. There was that twig-snapping sound again. The girls, all five of them, huddled closer.

"Be quiet!" I ordered, trying to sound more grown-up than I felt, but feeling younger than I really was. I made the girls join hands and get ready to run back into the cabin, when a rabbit almost as big as the Shephards' Great Dane leapt out of the thicket and disappeared in the grass on the other side of the clearing.

"Wow! He was cute," Edda said, laughing.

The highlight of the whole two weeks that I spent as a camp counselor was the second night, Sunday, when we built a camp fire and sang songs. I said that I hoped it'd get a little cooler in the woods, and it did. At night, it turned down right cold. I was extremely glad that Mama'd told me to bring my sweatshirt. I pulled the hood over my head and drew my hands up into the sleeves and sang along with the rest of them. Whoever said there's strength in numbers knew what they were talking about. If anything was out there lurking in the woods, our singing was gonna scare them away.

The next morning after breakfast, the groups went on a nature walk. It might've been a few degrees hotter that day. Anyhow, Miss Buckley got us up before sunrise, and by the time the walk got underway, the sun was beating down and feeling fiery hot.

We were all dressed alike in beige camp shorts and T-shirts with CAMP MUCKALUCK and the boots logo on it, even Miss Buckley, but she had on khaki slacks.

One thing about the nature walk. Boy! Did we

see nature! Miss Buckley pointed out blades of grass. "This is the basis for licorice candy. Pull off a blade and suck on it."

Of course, everybody pulled off a blade of grass and sucked it, even citified me. If you closed your eyes, you'd think you were sucking on licorice.

When we'd walked about twenty miles — Miss Buckley said it was a mile and a half — I would've given anything to be able to run upstairs and lie across my bed. I'd've given anything if the Shephards' Great Dane would chase me into my house again. The two weeks were moving like two years.

That afternoon, on the way back to camp again, Octavia slid down into a shallow ravine. Everybody scrambled down the hillock and helped her out. When we found out that she wasn't hurt, we all sat down in the ravine and rested. I could've spent the rest of the two weeks just sitting there and letting the breeze rustle through my hair and cool me off.

Fifteen minutes later, Miss Buckley said it was time to head back. Along the way, she pointed out interesting trees and shrubbery. She stopped up ahead — I couldn't help lagging behind with my group — and said, "This is poison ivy." I looked at the leaves. They were really pretty.

We still had a long ways to go before we reached the cabin. I kept peering around, then I spied a huge spider in a tree. It was the most frightful thing. I shudder even now when I think about it. I told the girls to hold hands, then we rushed through waist-high grass and into a clearing.

When we were in the clearing, I looked back. Miss Buckley had stopped and gathered the rest of the groups around. They were standing a few feet away from the spider. I heard Miss Buckley say, " — the wonders of nature — " But by the time she'd finished her sentence, my group and I were halfway to the cabin.

In that moment when I got sight of the cabin in the clearing, I thought it was the most beautiful building in the world. I couldn't believe that just three days before, I'd thought the cabin was the worst eyesore I'd ever seen. It wasn't home, but it'd have to do. For now.

All I wanted was a shower. But I couldn't take one until I saw that the girls in my group had taken theirs. I hoped Miss Buckley didn't have anything weird planned for that night. As far as I was concerned, we could sit around the camp fire and sing songs until it was time to go home. Or maybe tell stories. No ghost stories, though.

Miss Buckley did make a camp fire at dusk. We needed one real bad because it was chilly again. I sat huddled in my sweatshirt, trying not to think about the nature walk. The fire was nice, but it was attracting all sorts of flying and crawling things. And all of them seemed to flit straight at me. They attacked my face since the rest of me was covered.

Midway into story hour, a giant mosquito lit on my forehead. I swatted it, but the thing acted like it was stuck on with glue. I hit it squarely with the palm of my hand, squashed it as flat as a pancake. It felt as big as a bald eagle.

While I was sitting there listening to the kids tell stories, I knew I was going to write a letter to Mama. That very night, too. Even if I had to stay up all night.

Just then, two of the girls in my group got up and went around back. Still swatting bugs, I watched them go. I wondered if I ought to follow them, but before I could decide, they came back.

"Miranda, you want to use our insect repellent?" Octavia offered.

I wished I'd thought to bring some. "Thanks," I said, and took the pump bottle she handed me. I sprayed repellent on my palms and rubbed it on my face. "I hope this works."

But it didn't. The spray had made the bugs leave the other girls alone, but when I used it, bugs just swarmed around me more. It was like I'd sprayed on some kind of sauce to make my flesh tastier to the bugs.

That night before I went to bed, I sat at the little desk in the corner of the cabin and wrote to Mama. I read the letter over:

Dear Mama,

All is not well! Make up a story. Tell them anything. I was going to tell Miss Buckley that being in the woods makes me sick to my stomach. Could you tell her there's an illness in the family? Daniel Boone might've belonged out here, but I don't. Get me out of here! Thanks, Mama.

Love,
Miranda

I folded the letter and slipped it into an envelope. I had brought along some stamps. I stuck one on the letter.

The next morning, I gave the letter to Miss Buckley to mail when she went to the general store in a neighboring settlement. I felt kind of like Benedict Arnold must've felt passing secrets to the British, but I smiled when she stuck the letter, without looking at it, between a stack of other letters she had to mail.

Although I knew it'd take Mama a day to get my letter, I started watching the mail the very next day. I had sent a letter instead of calling because I secretly hoped that camp would get better. Anyway, I knew Mama was going to take her good old sweet time answering. She loved getting letters, but she hated writing them.

Surprisingly, Mama answered my letter posthaste. I almost snatched the letter from Miss Buckley as soon as I recognized all the extra loops and rattails in Mama's handwriting on the envelope. I tore it open and read:

Dear Miranda,
What have I told you about lying? I won't tell lies like that. Or, as you say, make up a story. Don't tell lies. You'll only get into trouble. Believe me, I know. Ordinarily, you're a good daughter. I didn't telephone because I thought you'd change your mind. By the time you get this note, if you're still set on coming home, call collect. But next time you go off on a tangent, I expect you to see it through.
　　　　　Love,
　　　　　Mama, AKA Justine Moses

Uh oh. I didn't like the tone of her letter. Reading between the lines, she sounded like she was getting ready to have a conniption fit. She must not've had a real good suspense thriller to read lately.

I started to write her another letter, but that would take too long. I went to the office and called her collect, just like she said.

The inside of the office looked like a hotel. A rural hotel way out in the middle of nowhere. It was wood-paneled in knotty pine. The floor was unfinished planks. You could almost get a splinter just from looking at it.

I went to the desk and picked up the phone and dialed. It took Mama a long time to answer. It was late enough in the afternoon for her to be home.

"Hello, Mama," I said when she'd finally picked up. "Daddy all right?"

She told me my father was great. Before she started giving me a lecture, I said, "Listen, I've decided to stay. Camp isn't so bad. I have only eight days. We're going to a clearing to collect rocks. We're going fishing on Thursday. We have different activities every day. We won't be going into deep woods again. Know what we're going to do for supper tonight? We're making beef stew from scratch. No, I'm not cooking it. I'm in charge of the camp fire and cleaning up. Did you know I know how to make a fire without a match? Just rub two sticks together. Tell Daddy hello, and I'll see you in eight days."

Around the camp fire that night, when we were eating the beef stew we'd cooked, one of the other counselors said, "Miranda, were you ever in the Girl Scouts?"

"No. Why?"

"The way you got that fire going. I would've still been rubbing those sticks together."

"It's easy," I said. "Only I think some of it was beginner's luck." I'd thought it'd be hard the way

Miss Buckley said to do it. I just rubbed the sticks real hard and fast.

"Yeah, right. I can barely make a fire with a match," the other counselor said.

We laughed. It's a good thing I didn't go home. I guess I just wasn't giving my job a chance.

The other counselor, her name is Renda, said, "This is great stew."

"Yeah," I said. "Food is always good when somebody else do the cooking."

Her eyes big and glowing from the firelight, Renda stared at me. She was chewing a mouthful of stew. She stopped in mid-chew, then started chewing again. After she'd swallowed, she burst out laughing.

"Miranda, you're all right," she said.

Since we didn't go trekking through the woods again, looking at nature, camp turned out to be great. Even if it hadn't been, I wasn't about to go home until my full two weeks were up. Not if it was going to give Mama the satisfaction of saying that I was a quitter. Besides, if I went home, it would seem like I was abandoning the little girls I was caring for. I had gotten attached to them over the past several days.

The last day at camp finally rolled around. Not that it looked like it took a long time. On Saturday morning, everybody got up at six and started packing. I threw my things back into the bags none too fussily. Most of them needed washing anyhow.

At eleven o'clock, we boarded the bus again and came home.

I knew I'd have to start looking for a job all over again, but that didn't matter. Maybe I'd find a job in an air-conditioned office just like Catriona Maryland. As I rode the bus, I could almost see her sitting in her office in a cool, crisp outfit, all starchy and stiff, and not even getting a single wrinkle by the end of the day. Why should she sit in an office, bug-free, and eat lunch in a real restaurant, and wear real clothes while I froze or baked in camp? Or served as breakfast, lunch, and a snack for everything that squiggled, crawled, crept, or flew around the camp?

The bus was almost in town before I realized maybe camp had been an excellent idea. I knew how to make a fire without a match. I'd eaten some great-tasting stew that I was going to have to try on Mama and Daddy since she insisted that I must cook. I'd learned some new songs. I knew which plants to avoid if I was lost in the woods. I'd made new friends. Renda and I had exchanged addresses. I was a few dollars closer to two pairs of contact lenses. I bet Catriona didn't know how to follow the North Star if she got lost in the woods at night. I laughed to myself then, because no matter how hard I tried, I couldn't picture Catriona Maryland trekking through the woods, night or day.

I closed my eyes, leaned back, and tried to think of other things. Different things. Anything other than Catriona or contact lenses, or even Teena, with her never-ending CD collection. I relaxed and listened to the rest of the kids chattering all the while the bus twisted and turned along the snaky highway. I must've dozed off, because when the bus drew up to the curb and stopped, I had some trouble remembering where I was.

FOURTEEN

It was around one-thirty that Saturday afternoon when I got home. Mama had gone to work, and Daddy showed up alone to drive me home. He was already there, waiting for me. I saw him out of the bus window before I'd pitched my things off the bus. He was wearing one of the navy blue uniforms he wore to his shop. With both hands in his pockets, he was leaning against the bus shelter wall.

He hugged me and grabbed my bags off the sidewalk. He hoisted them onto the back of the pickup truck. He did it with one hand as if my bags weighed only a pound or two.

We got into the truck, and off we went. I could barely wait to get home. I must've driven Daddy crazy rambling on and on about all the things I did at camp.

Pulling up into our driveway, he didn't shut the motor off but got out and took my bags upstairs. I was just easing into the house when he dashed back out again.

"Listen, honey. I hate to run like this, but I'm in the middle of a contract."

"Okay, Daddy," I said.

I went upstairs and put on a pair of slacks and a T-shirt and went back out to water the lawn. It looked like it needed it, bad. Read bad. I wanted to be outdoors some, look at the house, the yard, the neighborhood. Although I'd learned to enjoy camp, it was good to be back.

Although the sun wasn't very bright, it was extremely hot. I mostly let the hose wiggle on the lawn, sprinkling water everywhere, even on me. It felt cool and refreshing, wonderful, in fact. That afternoon, I was four years old again instead of fourteen. I had forgotten everything including wanting contact lenses to wear back to school in September. I had left my glasses upstairs on the bureau with a thousand of Teena's CDs. I didn't need glasses to romp and frolic in the water.

From the backyard next door, the Shephards' Great Dane looked at me. He was chained up. He sat on his haunches, his tongue lolling out, looking. He didn't let out a whimper. He didn't look so bold because I couldn't see him very well without my glasses.

I stood there in the backyard, soaking wet, my

slacks and T-shirt sticking to me and showing off curves I only imagined I had. Out of the corner of my eye, I saw movement along the sidewalk. I hoped it was Teena. I desperately wanted to talk to her. I had called her first thing, right after I'd changed my clothes. But I'd only gotten her mother.

Maybe she knew of some jobs. She was always up on things that were happening. Anyway, your best friend ought to come when you call. Ought to respond to your messages. I'd called four times since I'd been home.

I turned and looked toward the gate. The person I saw moving along the sidewalk was Catriona Maryland. She was licking an ice cream cone.

News of my homecoming had traveled fast and furious, like a forest fire, I thought, as I got ready to turn off the water.

The hose wiggled, zigzagged all over the yard, spewing water all over the lawn.

I went to the hydrant to turn off the water. Catriona moved into the yard. I stared at the hose. It wiggled more, wildly spraying water over the yard and everything in its path. It looped around and around like a toy balloon filled with air, then suddenly let go.

Catriona was standing just inside the gate, almost in range of the hose. She leapt back, but not fast enough. Each way she darted, the hose followed her, as if she were a magnet attracting it. I ran to the hydrant, turned the valve, but by then, Catriona was pretty well soaked. She was almost as drenched as I was.

I noticed she was still holding onto her ice cream cone. Water had splattered it and the melted ice cream trailed down her arm like creamy little rivers. I laughed.

Catriona was furious. Her face was wet, her blouse soaked so bad it looked gray instead of white. With the back of her hand, she wiped her face, smearing ice cream all over it.

"You did that on purpose, Miranda!"

I didn't deny it. "I'll get you some paper towels," I said, stifling another giggle. I went into the house. It was a pity Teena couldn't see this.

I brought the paper towels and handed them to Catriona. She took them, wiped her face, dabbed at her hair. Water had made her hair darker and shinier.

Through clenched teeth, Catriona hissed at me, "I'll get you for this. If it's the last thing I do."

What I couldn't see was why she was getting so mad. It was a hot day. The water felt good to me. I was lots wetter than she was. "If you try anything," I said, "it will be the last thing you do."

"You're just jealous of my job." She crumpled the paper towels and tossed them onto the well-watered lawn. She looked at the soggy, dripping ice cream cone still in her hand, as if it was a disgusting thing. She tossed it down on the edge of the walk.

"I'm not jealous of your job. I just think it was a bit underhanded the way you got it. Reverend Maryland pulled all kinds of strings — "

"He didn't!" she spat at me, cutting me off.

"Some needy teenager should've got that job."

"Like you, huh?" she sneered, dryly.

"No," I mumbled.

"We can't do a thing about that now, can we?"

Catriona was right. We couldn't do a thing about that. I know I couldn't. In a way, I was glad Mama had too much money.

"At least I got the jobs I had on my own," I said.

"You call baby-sitting and camping out jobs? If I wanted to go camping, I'd join the Girl Scouts," she said.

"The Girl Scouts wouldn't have you. You have to be truthful, loyal. Things you could never be."

"You're supposed to be so smart, you're the dumbest thing I ever saw."

Using both hands, Catriona pulled at her blouse as if she thought she could dump the water off it, make it dry again, I guess. Maybe she'd started feeling cold. I know I did. A wisp of a breeze had come up and in the one hundred-degree heat, I shivered.

"I'm going home. I bumped into your father in the shopping center and I came by to — welcome you back."

She turned around to leave. At the edge of the walk, she gave a swift kick at what was left of her ice cream cone, then moved on down the walk. The ice cream cone landed upside down on the lawn, on the other side of the walkway. It looked like a tiny Egyptian pyramid. I felt a little sad as I watched her go because I thought I'd actually missed her while I was at camp. I wished she was at camp — a prison camp. I watched until she turned the corner, then I went back to rolling up the hose. I went inside to change out of my wet clothes.

After I'd changed, I called Teena again. No answer.

FIFTEEN

"Where have you been?" I asked, when Teena finally showed up late Wednesday afternoon, four days later. Of course, she brought yet another CD. I groaned.

"Work — I — I was working. My aunt's been catering one party after another. And she's been running me ragged. She made me clean the walk-in freezer. Did you ever go in a walk-in freezer?"

I shook my head.

"You haven't lived till you been in one with a half a cow hanging on a meathook."

"A half a cow? Then I don't want to ever go in one," I said.

"I know you thinking they just keep ice cream in freezers, I bet."

"We keep all sorts of stuff in ours, even milk."

"Tell me about camp," Teena said. The new

109

CD was on my little red stereo, filling the room with music. The vibration from the sound knocked a few of Teena's old CDs to the floor. We let them stay there.

"What's to tell?" I said. "I didn't particularly like it. But I'm glad I stayed. It's just baby-sitting but with bugs, too. Oh, I liked the kids, though."

Teena sat on the foot of my bed slowly nodding. "Well, what're you gonna do now?"

"I don't know."

We sat there listening to the music for a while. Then I saw Teena's eyes light up, which meant she had an idea cooking.

"What? What?" I asked, anxiously.

"You're too young for this."

"Come on, tell me. Or else I'll make you stop using my CD player."

That didn't really faze Teena, but she did say, "My father says they're hiring at Produceland." She stopped and went to turn the volume down on the stereo. I thought about how her father drives a produce truck and would know about jobs at supermarkets and such like that.

"Why would I be too young?"

"You have to be sixteen at least. And you don't look anywhere near that."

I thought about how I'd just lied about my age on an application to become a camp counselor, and my age hadn't come up even once.

My face must've fallen because she said, "Don't

110

look like that. If you'd put on a little makeup, you could pass for fifteen or so."

"Teena, I *will* be fifteen in late September. And I don't want to wear makeup yet."

"Maybe you could just fix your hair differently."

I had always worn my hair loose and lightly curled. I guess because it's so thick, but maybe a new hairdo would help. It probably wouldn't hurt.

Teena and I practiced with my hair until it was time for her to leave, around seven o'clock. She fixed me a few new styles, but none of them really suited me. When I wanted to get dressed up, I usually wore my hair loose and that was the way I wore it to Produceland the first thing Thursday morning.

SIXTEEN

On Thursday morning, I got up at six-thirty. I'd tossed and turned most of the night anyhow, so I got up at first light. I took a shower in the downstairs bathroom so I wouldn't wake Mama. She had the day off because while I was at camp, she'd worked overtime on Sunday and instead of paying her extra money, they'd given her an extra day off. I'd already heard Daddy leave at six o'clock. I think Mama was glad to have a middle-of-the-week day off just so she could sleep. She couldn't sleep late on Sundays because she wanted to go to her church across town. On Mondays, she had to get up early to do things like washing and ironing uniforms and such like. Of course, we could've gone to Catriona's father's church since it was closer — four blocks up and around the corner, but we hardly ever went there.

I thought their congregation was too highfalutin'.

So while Mama slept in on Thursday, I got up and got ready to apply for a job at Produceland. I wore a suit. I put on a tiny touch of lipstick. That's all. And I wore my hair down.

At eight-fifteen, I walked into the shopping center to get the bus that would take me to Produceland.

When I got to the store and told the manager what I wanted to do, he said, "Kid, don't bother with this application if you ain't sixteen. You look twelve to me."

"I'm sixteen," I said, and reached out a brown hand for the application. When he didn't release it, I kept holding my hand out, ready to take it. I started feeling like a begger asking passersby for coins.

The manager — his name was Mr. Finelli — was young, too. He looked to be about twenty or so. He had dark curly hair and a thin mustache like he'd drawn it on with a pencil just this morning. He watched me a minute, grinned, then put the application into my hand. He turned back to other business on his desk.

Outside his office was a small window. There was a narrow counter, a shelf, really — at the window. I fished a felt-tipped pen out of my purse and stood at the little shelf and filled in the application. I tried to write neat but fancy, the way I thought a mature sixteen-year-old would.

I filled in all the blanks. When I got to the space that said "Age," I didn't hesitate a minute. I wrote in sixteen. It's funny how I've been saying and writing that number like mad lately, yet I hadn't choked on it. My pen hadn't broken, either.

On the back of the application at the bottom was a sentence, some kind of legal-sounding mumbo jumbo asking whether all the statements I'd made were true or not, but I just skimmed through it. Using bold strokes, I scrawled my name in the last blank space. I'd written my name in bigger letters than John Hancock had used when he signed the Declaration of Independence. I glanced at the application, then read it over once more, then handed it in.

"Thank you," I told Mr. Finelli, and smiled.

He took the application, looked it over to see if I'd left any spaces blank and said, "Okay. I'll get back to you in a few days."

A few days stretched into a week and a half. I had nearly given up when Mr. Finelli called. I was to work some mornings and three afternoons a week and never more than a total of twenty-eight hours. On Mondays, I was off just like Mama. My afternoon starting hours were noon to four. She was gonna love that. I'd get home just in time to cook supper. I didn't care right then. I had an honest-to-goodness real grown-up job.

I have to tell everything about my job. I was so very proud of it. I didn't do anything like get my folks to pull strings and say we were impoverished in order to get it. But I am a little ashamed of what I did, too.

That Thursday morning when I left the house, I kind of knew that this was the job for me at last. Even the smell of the place made me feel welcome. Produceland smelled like fresh sausages, celery, scallions, and delicious baked goods that I didn't have to cook! And the air conditioner was running full blast against the dog-day weather outside.

At the store, they'd given me handouts about how Produceland stays open twenty-four hours. I thought it was the cleanest, neatest store in the world. That was before they hired me. Afterwards, I trebled those sentiments. It was a joy to work there. Anything you wanted, they sold. They had two automatic teller machines, a Western Union outlet, a pharmacy that delivered, a bulk-food section, a garden shop, a hardware section, a basic sewing section, a video rental service. And, oh yes, they had a bookstore.

Without incident, I worked that first week in the produce section. It was my job to see that all the bins were stocked with plenty of fresh green and yellow vegetables and lots of fresh fruit.

I did the bananas all right, filled the bins, and Mr. Finelli showed me how to make a totem pole display of bananas. They were so golden ripe that they looked like they glowed. All of this had to be done without bruising them, of course.

On Friday of that week, when my shift was almost over, I looked up the aisle and saw a bony girl with close-cropped hair who looked surprisingly like Catriona Maryland. I sure didn't want to bump into her, as I still had all her threats hanging over me.

A new shipment of oranges had come in, and I was busy stacking them into the bins, making sure the older ones were on top and the new ones on the bottom. That's called rotating the stock. I wanted them to look attractive to the customers. I peered around the totem pole of bananas yet still tried to stack oranges. My hand must've slipped. I don't know exactly what happened. I don't remember because everything was happening so fast.

The next thing I knew, a billion oranges started falling, rolling, and going every which way on the floor. An orange landed with a splat right in front of one of the customers. She jumped out of the way and looked at me like I'd lost my last marble. I was more concerned about how I was going to get that mess cleaned up. I saw that other customers at the head of the aisle were turning their shopping carts around and going in a different direction.

Looking at the oranges again, I saw that there were only a few left in the display bins. But on the floor, it looked like the area in produce was carpeted with big juicy oranges. Mr. Finelli, naturally, had seen everything. From that little window, you have a clear view of the produce section.

Mr. Finelli grinned and rolled his eyes upward. Main thing, he didn't fire me. I bent and started picking up oranges. That's when my glasses fell off and landed smack-dab in the middle of the ocean of oranges. I couldn't see anything except one big orange smear, like someone had daubed the floor with gallons of bright orange paint. My face felt hot. I was too embarrassed to grope for my glasses. But grope I did until I found them and set them back on my face. I felt awkward and silly as if I was four years old instead of fourteen.

Since I could see clearly once more, I glanced at the office again. Mr. Finelli wasn't looking. If he had an ounce of decency in his body, he would've come over, taken me aside, and fired me. But he didn't. Fire me, I mean. The earth wouldn't open up and swallow me, either. Maybe when I got home, I could persuade Mama and Daddy to sell the house and we could move to some undeveloped country where they'd never heard of me or oranges. In the meantime, I went right on picking up oranges.

After I'd gotten the oranges back into the bin,

Mr. Finelli did come over, but all he said was, "You did a great job, a smash bang-up job. Until now."

I wished he wouldn't use smash and bang-up in the same sentence. I looked at the bins full of oranges. A few slid down a bit but didn't fall. Mr. Finelli looked at the displays, nodded, and went back to his office.

A customer pushed her shopping cart around to produce and said, "Gee, kid, you got 'em all picked up. I thought you were going to be here all evening."

She selected a bunch of bananas off the totem pole display, put it in her basket, snickered, then went away. I watched her disappear in the fresh flower section amid a jungle of ferns and rubber tree plants and whatever else they have in that section.

When I went to punch out at the end of my shift, Mr. Finelli still didn't fire me. All he said was, "See you tomorrow, Miranda."

"Good-bye, Mr. Finelli."

"Do you have to sound like you're not coming back?" he asked.

I gave a weak smile and said, "See you later."

"There. That's better."

Outside on the sidewalk, I hitched my purse on my shoulder, put my hands into the pockets of my jeans, and with my head hung, I went to catch the bus.

Please don't let it be my day to cook, I prayed silently as I waited. With my luck, I was scared I'd drop the food all over the kitchen floor and I'd have to mop, too.

I was lucky, because I didn't have long to stand in the sun and wait for the bus. When it came, I climbed on board and found a corner seat near the back, leaned my head against the window, and shut my eyes. Work was a lot harder than it looked. If I'd known what could've happened just by going to work, maybe I wouldn't've been so obsessed with finding a job. I thought about how bad I wanted contact lenses and tried not to think about what had happened. It was over, and I couldn't do anything about it now anyhow. I relaxed and leaned against the window until the bus drew up to my stop.

SEVENTEEN

Two weeks later, I got my first paycheck. Mr. Finelli handed them out at nine o'clock in the morning. He expected us to go on working as if nothing'd happened. Only thing, I couldn't. Oh, I still did my best, but I was always aware of my paycheck in my jeans pocket under my burgundy smock. During the course of the day, I must've patted my pocket a thousand times, making sure my paycheck was still there. It always was.

Naturally, one paycheck wasn't enough to go out and buy contact lenses. Even with me earning a little more than the minimum wage, I didn't have enough. I wanted to get off work and deposit my money into my savings account. I'd have to save until I got at least three more checks.

Although it took one o'clock a long time to come, it finally did. I went to the front of the store to the time clock to punch out. The time clock is pretty close to the door — up on the opposite side of the manager's office, and in walked Catriona Maryland. This time, it was really her, but I never would've thought she'd do ordinary things ordinary teenagers do, like shop for her folks. But there she was. What really bothered me about her was that she wasn't at work in the middle of a workday. Mornings I generally worked from nine till one. She worked at ten A.M. I don't know what time she got off. I think she worked six hours a day.

Up at the time clock, I was shrugging out of my smock and trying to get my time card into the clock without Catriona seeing me.

No such luck. The sound of the clock printing the time on my card echoed throughout the store. To my ears, it sounded as loud as a holdup man's gun.

As bad luck would have it, Catriona had just stepped off the automatic mat that opened the door as I was approaching the exit doors. "Miranda?" she said, her voice tentative, as if she couldn't believe what her eyes were showing her.

"Oh, hello, Catriona." I kept walking. I wanted to get to the bank and put my money in. Besides, not only was it my day to cook, but I still had Catriona's threats hanging over me. No telling what that sneaky old thing was gonna do.

"What are you doing here? Isn't that a Produceland smock? You're too young to work here. They wouldn't hire me and I'm a little older than you. I'm going to talk to the manager about you. I should've had a job here. I did apply."

Mr. Finelli was only about ten feet away in the office. He'd have to be as deaf as a doorknob not to have heard Catriona ranting and raving like a madwoman.

"You don't even look like you're old enough to work here — " She still wasn't finished.

"Why don't you shut up? You sound like an old broken record. I thought we decided not to have anything to do with each other anymore. Besides, you already got a job."

She stared at me from head to foot, then at the smock draped across my shoulder. My face was getting hot. Customers stared at us. "I've got to go," I said. I didn't want to leave Catriona there with Mr. Finelli, but I had to go. I didn't want to stay there and fight with her at the place where I worked. I looked down and saw that I was crumpling my smock. I'd crumpled it real bad. It'd need to be washed and ironed before I could wear it again. I started out of the store.

At the door, I turned and looked back and saw Catriona moving down the aisles, pushing her shopping cart as if she were in a relay race. She was moving faster than Flo Jo at the Olympics.

Back to the drawing board, I thought and went on out of the store. No matter what anybody said, my days at Produceland were numbered.

When I got home, I threw my purse on the chest of drawers. Slap, slap, slap! CDs started falling on the floor. Looked like five or six hundred must've fallen. I didn't care. My smock was really mussed up by now, since I'd crumpled it even more as I rode the bus home. The CDs stopped falling. I turned to go downstairs. Another CD fell. I went on downstairs.

In the kitchen, I pulled opened the refrigerator door and then the freezer, looking for something to cook for dinner. I must've been learning because Mama had stopped leaving little notes stuck around telling me what to fix. Now I had to find something to fix all by myself. Something the three of us might like. I looked over all the items in the freezer. Mama had them stacked as carefully as if they were in the freezer at Produceland.

Anyhow, that was one day I didn't really mind cooking. Not that I was glad, but it gave me something to do, something to occupy my mind. Trying to mix up the ingredients properly really did take my mind off everything that'd happened. After I got everything to cooking, I sat in the kitchen and kept my eye on the pots like a hawk. A watched pot *does* boil.

I wanted to call Teena and tell her what'd happened, but I couldn't. I didn't have enough energy and I was too mad. Besides, I was getting too deeply involved in making dinner. This was one dinner that was going to turn out perfectly even if I had to stand guard at the stove like a sentinel standing in front of the door of Fort Knox.

Later, when dinner was almost done, I did think about Catriona again. I just knew she'd gone back to the office after I'd left and told Mr. Finelli everything. I even gave some thought to what Teena'd said about working at Delightful Catering. But if I didn't like cooking at home, how was I going to do it for somebody else? Never mind that they paid me money. I wasn't about to change my mind about that. I decided the best thing — the only thing — I could do was go to Mr. Finelli's office first thing and tell him myself, beg for leniency or something. Maybe he wouldn't fire me. Maybe he wouldn't tell me never to darken Produceland's door again. Not even as a customer. If I had been the boss, I would've fired anybody who knocked oranges all around on the floor. Never mind that it was an accident.

By the time I got dinner finished, it was only four o'clock. If Mama came home talking about how I'd started cooking too early, I'd just remind her that all the seasonings had had a chance to go through the food.

When my folks came home, it was a quarter to six. I was still sitting in the kitchen mulling over the problems I had, when they walked in. I heard Mama's little car first, then Daddy pulled in right behind her in his silver pickup truck.

"Hi, you're home," Mama said, and grinned at me. She had a brown, wrinkled paper sack tucked under her arm. It was folded and looked like a book. Knowing Mama, that's what it probably was. "You've already fixed supper."

"Smells good in here," Daddy said, crossing in front of Mama and heading into the living room. "Soon's I wash up, I'm eating everything. Hope you made a lot."

While they were freshening up, I got the lasagna I'd made and set it in the center of the table. It was in a Pyrex baking dish and looked good from all sides. I hoped it'd taste good. It'd been in the oven about forty minutes, not only warming up, but I was trying to dry out some of the soupy tomato sauce. Mama's was never soupy. I heated the broccoli and put it into a bowl and set it on the table, too. I stacked slices of Italian bread onto a platter.

For a beverage, I was serving iced tea. I hadn't made dessert. Mama was gonna have a conniption fit, but I didn't care. There was about a quart of Neapolitan ice cream in the freezer. We could eat that.

After I got through telling them what was going on, they probably wouldn't even be able to eat the lasagna, let alone worry about dessert.

I stood back and admired the table. It looked

as good as a color picture layout in a food magazine.

At six-oh-five, we sat down to eat. There is a clock shaped like a sliced apple on the wall in the kitchen. I kept looking at it. Whenever it was my day to cook, I looked at the clock, wishing time would fly, I guess. But I was watching it now because I wished it were tomorrow and I'd already lived through this day.

I couldn't eat. Not a bite. Midway through the meal, Mama said, "Miranda, you're letting your broccoli get cold."

"Is something wrong?" Daddy asked.

Mama was right. I couldn't even eat my favorite vegetable. I sat there toying with my food. I wished I could've eaten the broccoli. They never would've known.

"There is a problem," I began, as I pushed a chunk of lasagna around on my plate. "I guess I can't blame anybody but me. I — " The rest of it stuck in my throat like a big hunk of lasagna.

"What's wrong? Something happened at Produceland? Did you get fired? Are you ill?"

"Justine, let the girl talk," my father said.

"But, Mike, I'm just trying — "

Daddy pushed up his glasses. Mama pushed up hers. I pushed up mine.

"You know the sentence at the bottom of a job application about all the statements being true — "

126

They nodded. Hesitantly, I went on. "I said I was sixteen years old." I shut my eyes and hung my head, waiting for them to start yelling.

"Oh, Miranda — " Mama said.

I was scared to tell them about Catriona's outburst at Produceland. I raised my head and looked at them. My parents looked so hurt sitting there trying to eat lasagna that I hadn't really wanted to cook in the first place.

"Go tell them the truth," Daddy said, simply. He would say that. He liked wearing glasses. I remember seeing him cleaning his glasses at the kitchen sink and polishing them up like they were the Hope Diamond or something. He took off his glasses, rubbed his eyes, and put them back on again.

"I — but — but — I might get fired," I stammered.

"You might get fired if you don't."

Mama said, "Getting fired will look a lot worse on another job application. Isn't that right, Mike?"

My father nodded. He had started back to eating. As far as he was concerned, the matter was settled.

"Listen, Miranda, honey, you've got a healthy mother and a reasonably healthy father — "

"What do you mean, 'a reasonably healthy father'?" Daddy said, peering over the top of his glasses at Mama.

She ignored him. "You mean all this came about because you want contact lenses?"

"Yes," I answered sadly.

Daddy sighed. Mama shook her head, sadly.

"May I be excused?" I said.

"Yes," Mama told me.

I eased out of the corner by the window air conditioner. I left my plate on the table and walked slowly out of the kitchen.

Halfway into the living room, I heard Mama say low to Daddy, "Mike, we couldn't spare that much money till the first of the year." I heard her scrape back her chair.

Slowly, I moved to the stairs and stood there, my hand on the newel post. I could still see into the kitchen. My father had his hand on Mama's arm so she wouldn't follow me.

"Leave her alone. She's going to get a job. Wait and see. She might not lose this one," my father said. "Whatever happens, she'll work this out. Wait and see."

Mama said, "Maybe it's too much for her."

"I don't think so," Daddy said. "Learning independence begins at home."

"That's charity," my mother said. "*Charity* begins at home."

"You know what I mean."

I climbed halfway up the stairs, out of range, so I'd stop eavesdropping. I looked back. I could still see the corner of the sofa. The book in the brown paper sack was still on the sofa where Mama'd left it. They couldn't even afford a new suspense thriller. Mama would've bought a new book if she could've. She went through them like a kid with a sweet tooth goes through a bag of candy. I wondered how ragged that book was.

That made me more determined than ever to go on working. I had to tell Mr. Finelli everything. Maybe I'd get another job right away. If worst came to worst, maybe I'd have to go down to Delightful Catering, although I didn't want that to happen. I went upstairs.

When I got to my room, I sprawled across my bed and stared at the ceiling. The answer to my problems wasn't up there, but I stared anyway.

Maybe Produceland would give me a good recommendation. I know one thing, my folks were right. My "confession" would sound better coming from me. I couldn't sit around and let Catriona spoil things for me. I couldn't blame her if she did. I couldn't blame her if she already had.

Although I wasn't due in to work until noon the next day, I almost called Produceland that very minute. But I decided it'd be best to say what I had to say face to face. First thing.

Since I'd mulled things over for a while, I did feel a little better. I went downstairs and finished eating. I ate all of my broccoli and almost finished the watery lasagna.

"Don't worry, honey," Daddy said.

They had already eaten a little something and were sitting there drinking coffee. I had made that, too.

Mama didn't say anything. She squeezed my hand, reassuringly. They drank their coffee.

"Are you going to be all right?" my father asked.

"I — I guess so."

He finished his coffee and went into the living room.

"You don't need help with the dishes?" Mama asked.

I knew she was anxious to get to the book she'd bought. I said, "No. I'll take care of them."

"Are you sure?"

"Yes," I said.

She went into the living room, then I heard her dump the book out of the brown paper sack. A few minutes later, I heard water running in the upstairs bathroom and I knew she was washing the cover of the book.

EIGHTEEN

On Saturday, I stayed in bed until ten-thirty. Mama was gonna have a conniption fit if she ever found out. She grew up on a farm and was used to getting up with the chickens, but since she and Daddy had both left around five-thirty or six, I just kept on lying there, trying not to think. And not being able to sleep, either.

At ten-thirty, I got up and took a bath and got dressed. I had to be at work by high noon.

It was eleven fifty-seven when I walked into Produceland. I went and stuck my card in the time clock and went to my station to work. That day, it was my job to dust off bottles and canned goods with a feather duster. I started doing that. You'd think that with everything lined up neatly, there'd be no dust, but it's amazing, I could've written my name in the dust on the shelves and on top of the canned goods.

On my afternoon break at one-fifteen, I caught Mr. Finelli in his office and confessed everything. I didn't leave anything out.

When I had finished, we were silent. It looked like the whole store got quiet. Saturday is the biggest day at a supermarket, but I don't remember even hearing the *beep beep* of the cash registers, or mothers chastising their children. Or children yelling, babies crying. Nothing. Just a scary quietness. Like when you're baby-sitting and you leave two children in a room and they get as quiet as a stone. Then, you go to them and find out they've done something terrible.

Suddenly, Mr. Finelli started talking. It seemed like he'd opened his mouth and words wouldn't stop coming out.

"My grandfather started this store many, many years ago," Mr. Finelli said. "He worked as a janitor at night, and sold fruits and vegetables from a pushcart by day until he got enough money.

"The story I hear in my family is that my grandmother wanted my grandfather to stay home during the day and get some sleep. Of course, he wouldn't hear of it. She said, 'All right, go to your produceland.' " His story must've brought back a lot of pleasant memories. He smiled broadly, then went on. "He was going to call his store

Produceland whenever he got it. So, that's it."

"That's a nice story, Mr. Finelli," I said as I wondered why he was telling it to me.

"We haven't had many a worker like you. Some, but not a whole slew. You're always on time. When your fifteen minutes' break is over, you come back to work. You always do as you're told. You're a very good worker. You kind of remind me of my grandfather, Miranda. In the best possible way. You're very determined. He told me once, 'You don't hold a job, it holds you.'

"I appreciate you coming in and telling me like this. And I hate to do it. I wish that there was another way out. There are labor laws — " He faltered.

"Yes, I know, Mr. Finelli." He pulled my file, studied it.

"Listen, Miranda," he said, "in a year you will be sixteen. If you still want the job, will you come back?"

I couldn't speak. I'd expected him to be angry that I'd deceived him, that I'd lied. My tongue stuck to the roof of my mouth. I tried to unstick it so I could talk. I couldn't. My head bobbed up and down like I had a coiled spring in my neck.

"A year isn't a long time. It'll probably seem that way because you're so very young. But these few months'll fly by before you know it." He ran a hand through his dark hair, his fingers mussing the curls.

"Thanks, Mr. Finelli." I stood up, started to leave. I went to the time clock, got my card.

Mr. Finelli looked at me, his eyes as big as two fifty-cent pieces. They were bigger than my own eyes magnified through the thick lenses of my glasses.

"I-I'm leaving."

"No, you don't. You can work until the end of your shift today. That way, you'll get another day's pay. Of course, if you feel you wanna leave — " He left the words hanging. I put my card back into the slot and went back to work. My fifteen minutes' break was over.

The last few hours I worked in the bookstore section. I looked at the rows and rows of books, some best-sellers, others just there. I had to stack them neatly, dust them off. People would come in and remove the jackets just to see how the book looked without it, I guess. Mama did that sometimes, too. But customers at Produceland sometimes wouldn't put the dust jackets back onto the books. I got everything shipshape, which wasn't a small job with the thousands of books there. Then, it was time to go home.

It's the weirdest thing to get fired. I don't know what'd happened in my case. Was I fired or did I quit? Whatever had happened, I didn't have a job anymore.

Getting fired must be like breaking up with a

boyfriend you really liked a lot. I felt hurt and ashamed at the same time. It seemed like when I walked out of the store, people were going to point and say, "There goes Miranda. She's a good worker, but she lies."

At the time clock, I pulled off my Produceland smock, draped it across my purse. I stuck my time card into the clock. The clock struck it, echoing throughout the store.

I went out of Produceland and walked to the corner to the bus stop. Nobody pointed. Nobody said a word.

NINETEEN

I still hadn't found another job by the end of the next week. The week after that, either. I wasn't giving up hope, yet discouragement was trying to creep in. So, on Thursday of the third week after "quitting" at Produceland, I went out job hunting again. I didn't find anything. And, to make bad matters worse, it was my day to cook. Since I didn't spend part of the day working, I had plenty of time to plan the meals. Mama must've realized this, because she let me choose what to cook, too.

She had left a ten-dollar bill on the dining room table. With it was a note she'd scrawled that said GO GET SUPPER! on one of those sheets of paper from the hospital memo pad. Looking back, I should've waited until she and Daddy got home and called out for a pizza. That's what I would've done at the beginning of the summer. I still hadn't learned to love cooking, or even like it, but doing it would give me something to occupy my time. I wouldn't worry about not having a job. Or being so close to a pair of contact lenses that I could almost smell the saline solution I'd have to wash them in.

I balled up the note from Mama, pitched it into the kitchen garbage can, then headed for Produceland. I had to go there if I wanted to get something balanced for the three of us. At a supermarket, you can always buy house brands and stuff on special and stretch that ten dollars like a rubber band.

Around five-thirty, after I'd shopped and was fixing dinner, Teena came over. Mama was in the living room reading a ragged old suspense thriller that she complained not only smelled moldly, but had too much modern technology for her to understand. But, since she'd spent the fifty cents for it, she had to finish it. Mama never started anything she didn't finish.

Teena sat in the kitchen watching me fix dinner. She said, "Miranda, I'm so glad to be away from that place. My aunt was in a real snit. Some advertising agency wanted to charge her an arm and a leg to write something she could use in the ad she's going to place in the paper at the end of the month.

"Girl, she's been tearing her hair out over that

for the past two days. She even offered the cooks and the other workers some extra money if they'd help her."

"Did they?" I asked as I lifted the lid and peeked into the pot.

"Naw," Teena said.

"She sounds like me. I can't seem to find another job, either. I left the money I earned working at Produceland and camp in the bank. But it still looks like I won't ever get my contact lenses."

"Can't you even get just one pair?" Teena asked.

"That'd take a lot of money, too. I have to pay for the doctor's exam, insurance. Everything. I might as well do it right if I'm gonna do it at all."

I went back to the stove and stirred in the pot some more. Steam swirled around my face, fogging up my glasses almost before I had the lid off. I wiped my glasses on my apron, smearing them, and slammed the lid back on the pot.

"You still getting your mother a suspense thriller?"

"I don't know. Not if I don't find a way to get the rest of the money I need."

"Don't worry, you'll get it. You'll get another job."

"When?" I had to ask. She sounded more confident about me getting a job than I did. I thought she knew something I didn't.

"I don't know the answer to that," Teena said.

"Whatever you're cooking sure smells good."

"Chicken noodle soup," I said. "I found the recipe in one of Mama's cookbooks. It didn't sound too complicated. Besides, all I really had to buy was a chicken and celery and the noodles. I bought a package of Jell-O for dessert. Can you stay?"

"No. I sure would like to. That soup smells so good. But I've got a long day at Aunt Delight's tomorrow."

Teena left soon after. I made some corn muffins to go with the soup. They could have a salad, too, if they wanted it.

When the muffins were done, I yelled into the living room to let Mama know she could eat if she was hungry.

"I'm going to wait for your father," Mama said.

"Okay, I'll wait, too." I made sure the fire was turned off, then went upstairs.

First thing I did was turn on my stereo. I turned it low, and soft music filled the room. I sprawled across my bed facing the stereo. Although I hadn't been able to master playing the drums and get into the school band, I still loved music. Not enough to invest all my money in CDs. If I had a CD in the bank, I could go cash that thing and get my contact lenses. But I didn't have anything in the bank except the money I'd earned at camp and working at Produceland.

I lay there staring at my stereo. It didn't look

secondhand at all. When I first got it, it'd been missing several knobs, but Daddy had found some replacements and it looked almost brand-new. All I had to do was wipe some of the dust off it.

But could I sell it? Was it worth enough money? Nobody knew it was used except my folks. And a clerk somewhere in a used furniture store. How much had my folks paid for it any-how?

Maybe I could just pawn it. Did I need to be eighteen for that? I laughed out loud thinking of the times I'd tried to pass for sixteen. Eighteen was really stretching it.

All those things reeled around in my fourteen-year-old desperate brain. Then I thought of how Mama and Daddy had looked when they'd given me the stereo for my last birthday. How they'd grinned all over themselves, how very, very happy they had been. Almost as happy as I'd been.

No, I thought. I could never sell my stereo. I couldn't even pawn it, although I could get it back when I found another job. If I found another job. That was just too much to deal with. Besides, they'd notice that the stereo was gone. Maybe Mama would really have a conniption fit, but any-way, I didn't want to hurt their feelings.

I had to keep hoping that I'd find a job soon.

Real soon. The thing to do was to keep trying, just like Teena had said.

Mama and Daddy would've bought me contact lenses if they could've spared the money. They did have the house payments, car and truck payments, food, clothing, and heating bills, telephone bills. Everything I thought they had to pay collided in my head, not only giving me a headache, but making me wonder if they had any money at all. I began to wonder if they even had as much money in the bank as I did.

I stayed sprawled on the bed listening to the music. I thought about going down to the supermarket to see if any baby-sitting jobs were up. I vetoed that idea because it'd take too long. I didn't move. I listened to the music.

Suddenly, over in the yard of the house next door, the Shephards' Great Dane started yowling. At first it was soft, sounded so far away. It had to be the Shephards' dog, because the Peters on the other side of our house had a couple of cats.

The Great Dane went on yowling. I started to wonder what was the matter with him. I pulled up off the bed and went to the window.

Drawing back the curtain and looking out, I saw that the Great Dane was trying to jump the fence. Not out of his yard into ours the way he usually did, but get out of the Shephards' yard. Maybe he was tired of being fenced in.

I let the curtain fall back into place, then went down the hall to the bathroom and washed my hands and face. I went downstairs.

Standing at the window in my room, I had made a decision. I didn't know if it was going to work or not. All I know is that I had to do something. I had already come too far to not do anything else.

There was still plenty of daylight left. Sunlight streamed in through the dining room window. There was still time to do what I had decided to do. Anyway, it would have to wait until after supper.

I heated up the food and by the time it was ready, Daddy came in.

"Hello, honey, you still fixing supper?"

"Hi, Daddy," I said.

"It smells like some kind of soup."

"That's what I made," I said. I went and set the table.

We ate quietly. At least, I did. Mama and Daddy chattered on and on as if they hadn't seen each other in ages.

The soup wasn't bad. It was probably even better. My father had two bowls, and Mama could only finish one and a half. I didn't bother. I wanted to clear the table and see if my decision was a good one.

TWENTY

After supper, Mama and Daddy went into the dining room. They sat to the table, a stack of bills in front of them. They were using the natural light to see while they looked over the bills.

I filled the sink with water, squirted in some lemon-scented dish detergent, and turned off the water. I would wash them later. I dried my hands on a paper towel, then went out.

On the Shephards' doorstep, I took a deep breath and rang their doorbell. I stood there waiting and realized I didn't even know the Great Dane's name. Maybe he didn't even have one.

The Shephards were taking so long to answer, I was about to leave, about to go home and wash dishes, but then Mr. and Mrs. Shephard stood there, smiling. They both wore rimless eyeglasses that were set low on their noses. They looked like brother and sister instead of an old married couple.

"Ah, Miranda," Mrs. Shephard said.

"Hello, Mr. Shephard, Mrs. Shephard," I said, and smiled, and kept one eye open for the Great Dane.

"What's on your mind, Miranda?" Mr. Shephard said.

"I'm starting a dog-walking service in the neighborhood — "

Mrs. Shephard's face crinkled up even more into a broader smile. She said, "Oh, Miranda, that's wonderful. It's good to have an entrepreneur in the neighborhood."

"And right next door, too," Mr. Shephard agreed. "Do you mind walking our dog? I got the feeling you were scared of her."

"Me, scared?" I asked. "He looks like a good little puppy," I added, almost choking for calling a dog that big a puppy. Anyway, I had to start with him. If I could walk the Shephards' Great Dane, I could do anything.

"She," Mrs. Shephard said. "Blossom's a she."

"How are your rates?" Mr. Shephard wanted to know.

I told him how much I charged.

"Well. Whatever, she's worth it. I'll get her leash." They stepped back into the house. "Come on in."

I went in, and Mr. Shephard closed the door.

Their air conditioner was blasting. They must've had a stronger one than we did, because their house felt as cold as a freezer.

Mr. Shephard came back with the Great Dane — Blossom — on the end of the leash. Blossom didn't look so scary with Mr. Shephard holding the leash like that, but she still looked big. She looked too big for the Shephards' living room.

"Take good care of her, Miranda," Mr. Shephard said, and put the leash into my hand.

Before I could grasp the leash, the Great Dane leapt against me and knocked me flat on the Shephards' living room floor.

"Down, Blossom!" Mrs. Shephard commanded, clapping her hands.

Blossom, nothing, I thought. That dog need a name like Killer, or Tank, or Dracula. Never mind that it was female.

Blossom obediently got off me. Mrs. Shephard grabbed the leash and pulled the dog over to the side of the living room and told Blossom, "Mind Miranda. Roy and I can't get around to walk you like we used to."

So Blossom and I walked around the neighborhood. I took her up the hill to Teena's house.

Teena and her mother were sitting out in the backyard under the big maple tree, cooling off. "Hey, Teena!" I yelled. She came around the side of the house and came through the gate.

"Oh, you made friends with the Shephards' dog," she said, grinning. Her teeth flashed in the dwindling sunlight.

"More than that," I said. "I'm earning extra money, too."

"A dog-walking service. We didn't even think of that."

"I think I'll have some business cards made up."

"Good idea," she said.

"You want to walk with us?"

Teena looked around. Her mother was lying on the chaise lounge reading a magazine. "Momma," Teena hollered, "I'll be right back. I'm going with Miranda."

"Okay. Be careful," Mrs. Mayson said.

Teena slammed the gate shut and we left.

"You can cut up some index cards and make your own business cards," she said as we almost trotted trying to keep up with Blossom. "That sure is a big dog. 'Specially seeing him up close like this."

"Her," I corrected. "Can you believe they named this dog Blossom?"

Teena laughed. "Godzilla would've been better."

"D'you think enough people want their dogs walked?"

"Yeah. Once you get the cards fixed up, you'll find out for sure. The other week, the Wainwrights next door to me wanted me to walk their poodle. I was on my way to work. Their dog barks like he'll bite."

"They say a barking dog won't bite," I told her.

"Yet and still, I won't take a chance. Only a dead dog won't bite anyway."

All the while we walked Blossom, Teena and I talked about my plans for the new dog-walking service.

"When I take Blossom home, will you come and help me make up some business cards?"

"Tonight?"

We were in the park near Teena's house. Old Blossom pulling us along. At least, pulling me along. I held onto the leash so she wouldn't get away. Teena had to stride to keep up with us.

She stopped. She looked worried. "I don't know, Miranda."

"Please," I said. I knew she didn't like to be out after dark, but it was only eight o'clock. The sun didn't look like it'd set. Not before quarter to nine, at least.

I looked at Teena. She was leaning against the chain link fence around the park, her hands in the pockets of her cut-off jeans. A breeze made the collar of her blouse flap up and down. It was a little cooler that evening.

Blossom leapt up and down in the grass. I held onto the leash.

I've never known Teena to hesitate so long.

Maybe she was still thinking about her house being burglarized.

"You can leave before dark," I said.

She nodded, then said, "Okay. I'll do it."

Blossom stopped jumping around and started sniffing at a clump of grass. I jerked the leash ever so slightly. "Okay, Blossom, girl, time to head back."

Teena waited while I gave Blossom back to the Shephards.

"Isn't it weird," I said when we were going up the walk to my house, "the Shephards have a Great Dane instead of a German shepherd?"

She laughed, then said, "They say people start looking like their pets. With those big sad eyes and short dark fur, old Blossom does resemble the Shephards."

I laughed and fished the front door key out of the pocket of my shorts. I unlocked the door and we went in.

TWENTY-ONE

In my room, I cleared off the top of my desk. I put the vase I kept pens and pencils in on the foot of my bed. I set my portable typewriter on the floor by the desk. It was the same typewriter Mama had used when she was going to college to become a dietitian. It was a little outdated, but it still typed just fine.

After the desk was cleared, I went out into the hallway near Mama's room and dragged in an old upholstered stool Mama had bought at Goodwill. I brought the stool into my room so Teena could sit at the desk with me.

"Teena, listen. Let's not do business cards. I think flyers. I can put them under windshields, hook them onto screen doors, put them everywhere. They're bigger. Everybody'll be able to see them."

"Yeah," Teena said. "That's even better."

I got some tying paper, handed it to her. She's good at sketching and lettering. I let her have the desk chair while she worked. I drew the stool closer to the desk and watched.

"You don't mind if I watch, do you?"

"Be my guest," she said as she took a sheet of paper from the stack and started working.

We were quiet while Teena worked. The only sounds were the *skrit skrit* her marking pen made as she scratched her sketches on the sheet of paper.

Suddenly she stopped and said, "You're going to make a lot of money. 'Cause you can walk more than one dog at a time."

I hadn't really thought much about how I would do it. I just wanted to earn the money myself. All of it. I said, "I hope you're right."

She'd already gone back to sketching on the sheet of typing paper. After a few more strokes, she capped the pen. I heard the top snap on in the quiet room. It felt strange to sit in my room without listening to a CD. This was the first time in a long time that she hadn't brought a new CD. "Look at this," she said, holding up the sheet of paper away from us at arm's length.

"It looks great," I told her. I took the sheet of paper and looked at it from another angle. "This is exactly what I was thinking about."

She had sketched a dog that looked like a poodle in the left-hand corner of the paper. At the bottom was a very good sketch of Blossom. Across the top of the page she'd written my name in calligraphic letters, and in much smaller letters below it she'd written "dog-walking service." Across the bottom, she'd written my telephone number. It was big, too, but not as big as my name.

"I'm gonna run those off at the copy center and pass them out around the neighborhood. Maybe I'll get a deal at one of those places that charge four cents a page."

Teena wasn't listening. She was peering out of the window on the other side of the room. Toward the Shephards' house.

"Miranda, it's getting dark. I'd better go." She got up.

At the door, she turned and said, "I don't have to be to work until twelve. I'm sleeping till eleven at least."

"That isn't sleeping," I told her. "That's hibernating."

She laughed and went downstairs. I heard her say good night to my folks and the front door open and close again.

The next morning at eight o'clock — some things I don't put off, either, just like Mama — I was on my way to the photocopy center to copy my flyer.

151

On the corner, a block from my house, I was waiting for the light to change when a big blue Cadillac drew up to the curb and stopped. I leaned over and peered into the car. It was Mrs. Maryland and her daughter, Catriona. Mrs. Maryland smiled. Catriona sat silently, staring straight ahead. She didn't even turn to look in my direction. I don't know what was wrong with her. I hadn't done anything to her lately. Of course, I still felt like I had her threats hanging over me. You could never tell what Catriona was going to do.

"Hello, Miranda," Mrs. Maryland said. "I don't know where you're going, but we're going all the way downtown. You're welcome to ride with us."

"Thanks," I said. I went around and opened the door. It was a two-door sedan with a padded top.

Grudgingly, Catriona slid over about a fraction of an inch. I got in.

"Miranda, she isn't mad at you. We had a little spat." She turned to face Catriona and said, "Catey, scoot over this way some more. As slender as you two girls are, there's plenty of room."

Catriona scooted over some more. Of course, I could've gotten into the back.

When we had moved out into traffic again, Mrs. Maryland said, "Catriona tells me you lost your job."

"Yes, ma'am. I'm starting something new today." I didn't know what I was going to say if she wanted to know more about it. I didn't feel like telling her what I was really going to do. Later, maybe I'd take a flyer up to their church and put it on the bulletin board.

Mrs. Maryland nodded, her eyes on the street. There wasn't a lot of traffic in our section of town that early in the morning.

"That's good," she said.

We crept along the streets. Mrs. Maryland didn't drive fast at all. Mama would have been zipping along in her little car.

Twenty minutes later, I got out on Fifth and Smithfield. I walked the two blocks up Smithfield to the photocopy center. The clerk told me it'd take about a half hour. There were plastic chairs lined up against the window. I could've waited there until my flyers were ready. But I felt like getting a cup of coffee and a Danish.

I didn't move right then because I was staring out of the window. I saw Catriona and Mrs. Maryland coming down Forbes. Mrs. Maryland swung the car back around to Smithfield Avenue, then stopped. Catriona got out. Mrs. Maryland had stopped the car in the bus lane. I saw Catriona move up the street toward the office where she worked.

I glanced at the copy center clock. Two whole minutes had inched by since I'd given them the flyer I wanted copied. I couldn't stay there. Waiting was making me too nervous. I walked out of the copy center.

At the corner, I bought a morning newspaper from a street vendor. I went to a restaurant and ordered a small coffee and a cheese Danish. Cream and sugar were already on the table. I put some into my coffee and bit into my Danish.

This delicious meal had taken a dollar and twenty-four cents off my contact lens money. Photocopying the flyer woud take another four dollars and thirty-four cents. It didn't matter now. I picked up the newspaper, opened it out, and searched for the comics. Maybe they'd take my mind off money while my coffee got cool enough for me to drink.

I was holding the paper up, reading the funnies, and didn't see Catriona and her mother come in.

By rights, I should've left after I realized that they were there, but it was still too early to check on my flyers.

The Marylands had taken a seat at a table in the back of the restaurant. I could hear them talking, but I don't think they could see me. There was a dry sink with plastic flowers separating my table from theirs. I wasn't really paying much attention to them.

I was trying to figure out what *The Far Side* meant when Mrs. Maryland said, "This is the first paycheck we've had in a — "

"I know. You told me once, Mother," Catriona said, cutting her mother off.

"Why can't you be a good little daughter like Miranda and her little friend — ?"

"Them two looney tunes? Little Teena, as you call her, too scared to buy a new CD player. Them crooks stole hers way back last March. I would've bought fifty by now. And Miranda — "

I squashed my newspaper and slid out of the chair. Of all the nerve! I thought. She couldn't talk about my friend like that. And no telling what she was getting ready to say about me. I bet she'd change her tune if somebody broke into her house.

Halfway back to the copy center, I was trying to remember something Mrs. Maryland had said. I was at the corner, waiting for the light to change. I wished I could remember. I searched my brain. I wished I'd listened more closely. Anybody else would've been all into their conversation.

The light changed. Still, I didn't cross the street. Early morning shoppers walked past me. I stood there, trying to think.

I started across the street. In the middle of the crosswalk, I remembered. Mrs. Maryland had said, "This is the first paycheck — " Whose paycheck? Catriona's? That meant that Catriona's father probably hadn't been able to pull strings, even if he had approached Mrs. Storm at the beginning to get his daughter preferential treatment or maybe just a good job. Some of the kids in the summer jobs program were working in the streets, cleaning them, or cleaning vacant lots. Even cutting grass. But Catriona wouldn't've done that in a million years. Even if it paid five hundred dollars a day. That just meant the Marylands didn't have any money at all. Or not a lot.

I spent most of the day placing my flyers all over the neighborhood. I'd already gotten a couple of calls by the time Mama came home that afternoon.

Mama wasn't shocked like I thought she'd be when I told her what I'd heard. I said, "They're just pretending. All of them. Even their skinny old daughter."

"Now, Miranda, honey, don't judge. I guess they're just trying to live their lives. That's all anybody can do. This is probably the only way they know how."

"Yeah, but I wish Catriona wouldn't put on airs so much. I was even planning on inviting her to Teena's birthday dinner."

Mama was cooking — it was her day. She bustled about the kitchen, working so confidently. I wondered when I'd get self-assured like that, or if I ever would.

"You can still invite her."

"No, I can't. Not after those awful things she

said about Teena. And, who knows what she was going to say about me?"

"I still think you should ask her. I think she sounds like a very lonely young girl."

Mama was expertly grating cheese for a salad she was making. I would've grated a finger or two if I had been doing it as fast as she was.

Mama said, "Just ask her, Miranda."

"Oh, okay," I said. "But she's just one snooty girl if you ask me."

"Well, that's just the way it is," Mama said.

TWENTY-TWO

On Monday morning, while Mama was sleeping in on her day off, I got up at eight o'clock and walked the Wainwrights' poodle. He didn't bite me. Teena had been worried for nothing. The Wainwrights' poodle really was a good little puppy.

I stayed out with him a long time because people kept stopping to admire him. They all thought he was my dog until I told them about my dog-walking service. I got a lot of requests, too. I knew that in a few days, I'd have more than enough money to pay for my own contact lenses. I could definitely buy Mama a brand-new, hot-off-the-presses suspense thriller.

Later that afternoon, I walked five dogs at once. The leashes got tangled once in a while, but all went well. I kinda thought the dogs would start fighting, but they didn't. I don't know what I would've done if they had. I wasn't going to worry about that yet. Not until it happened.

So I got the dogs walked and took them to their homes. It was my day to cook and I had no idea what I was going to make. It had to be something easy, something that wasn't going to take all night. Ordinarily, we ate around six or seven. With me getting such a late start, we'd be lucky to eat at quarter till eight.

By the time I got home, my mind was still a complete blank. I even toyed with the idea of calling out for pizza. I vetoed the idea. I had misgivings about the dollar and twenty-four I'd spent on fast food last week. It was cheaper to cook something. All this thinking about money was making me halfway crazy.

At least, I thought, I wouldn't have to go to the store. Mama had taken it upon herself to go grocery shopping on Saturday after she got off work. I wished she'd slip up and cook on my day. Just once. But I knew she wouldn't. She kept up with the days we cooked as closely as she did the patients' diets at the hospital where she worked.

I unlocked the door and went in, hoping to smell food cooking. No such luck. The house didn't smell like anything. I went into the kitchen and slumped into a chair. Now I know how Daddy feels, I thought. Having your own business is a lot of work. I glanced at the apple clock. It was getting late. I had to make something before Daddy came home.

Suddenly, I leapt up. If Mama had bought some of those hamburgers already shaped — she sometimes did. She thought they saved time.

I yanked open the refrigerator door. There they were. I left them there and got some potatoes peeled, diced them, and put them into a pot to boil on the stove. I threw a few eggs into the water. Potato salad, hamburgers, and chocolate pudding. Slap the potato salad on a lettuce leaf, slice onions and tomatoes for the hamburgers. Open a jar of hamburger dill pickle chips. All of this a balanced meal. Even the greatest dietitian in the world couldn't find fault with it.

I stripped a head of letttuce, washed it. Then sliced some tomatoes and onions. I put all of this into separate bowls, covered it, and set it back into the refrigerator.

When the potatoes were done, I cooled them off fast by draining them in a colander and running cold water over them. Then, I put the hamburgers on. While they were cooking, I sat to the kitchen table with a notepad and a felt-tipped pen and made plans for Teena's birthday dinner.

"Maybe you'll consider cooking all the time," Mama said when she'd finished eating. "That was good potato salad. Nice and cold. Just the way I like it."

"Thanks," I said.

"How's the dog-walking service?" my father wanted to know.

"Great!" I said. "I'm going to get my contact lenses on Thursday morning. First thing."

They sat there sipping coffee and eating cold potato salad and grinning and winking at each other. You'd think I'd said I was going to buy them their dream house, or pay that mountain of bills or something.

After I'd cleaned the kitchen, I went upstairs and counted my money. Then I took a shower and went to bed.

TWENTY-THREE

On Thursday, my appointment was for nine o'clock. At eight forty-seven, I was already seated in the doctor's office, leafing through magazines. I didn't really pay any attention to what was printed on the pages in the magazines. I mostly sat there nervously pushing up my glasses. They'd gotten a lot looser since the beginning of summer and I was glad to finally give them up.

I flung the magazine aside and just sat there waiting my turn. I wished it was already over with and I could go home.

At nine o'clock sharp, the receptionist ushered me into the inner office.

By eleven o'clock, I walked out of the doctor's office wearing my new contact lenses, bought and paid for with my own money. Money I'd earned myself. For some reason, I felt lighter as I walked to the bus stop. My old glasses were tucked into an inside pocket in my purse along with the instructions on how to care for my new contact lenses.

"You've got them," Mama said, grinning all over herself as I went into the house and through the living room, headed for my room. "Let me look at you."

I stopped, my hand on the newel post, ready to go upstairs. I turned and looked at her. I smiled.

She stared at me for the longest time, smiling all the while. She was clutching a ragged old suspense thriller. "I want to see them when you take them out," she said.

Up in my room, after I'd stopped looking in the mirror, I went to my desk and looked over the guest list for Teena's birthday dinner. While I studied the list, I reached up a thousand times to push up my glasses, then I'd remember I was wearing contact lenses.

Satisfied with the guest list, I got a paper clip and clipped the menu to the list. Menu? I was really turning into a cook. Or else beginning to sound like Mama.

The list and the menu were printed on two 4 × 5 index cards. I propped it against the vase that I kept pens and pencils in. I went downstairs.

"Mama, Teena's party is next Saturday. Daddy'll be here, won't he?"

"Yes," Mama said, without looking up from her suspense thriller.

I wanted to tell her that I was going to make baked beans from scratch, but I let her go on reading. It'd be a surprise. If they turned out perfectly, then I'd be surprised, too.

Suddenly Mama looked up. She said, "You look really nice, Miranda. Did I tell you before?"

She sat in the big blue corduroy chair by the window. She rubbed a slender-fingered brown hand over the cover of the book she was holding. "You did remember Catriona?"

How could I forget, I thought, but what I said was, "Of course."

Of course I wanted to forget, but I thought about having a cookout instead of an indoor dinner for Teena. I could make a green salad, grill some 'burgers and hot dogs, and make a big bowl of punch.

"I'll go make sure her name's on the list right now," I told Mama, and went back upstairs.

Sitting to my desk, I made plans for this last week before Labor Day. Pretty soon, school would be starting again, and I wanted Teena's birthday dinner to be a special event for the end of summer.

On the twenty-seventh, I could go shopping, and since that was my day to cook, I could start cooking the baked beans a day early and keep them in the refrigerator. All the seasonings would have time to go through them. It was going to take a long time to cook baked beans anyhow. I could start them while I was cooking supper on the twenty-seventh. I'd probably have to simmer them all the while Mama and Daddy and I were eating supper. Maybe even longer.

That night, before I went to bed, I took my contact lenses out, cleaned them, and took them and showed them to Mama.

"Fish eyes. They look like fish eyes," she said.

I thought they looked like two raindrops. Two half raindrops, at least.

Steadily, for the next couple of days, I got a lot of customers for my dog-walking business. I was usually pretty well tuckered out by the time I was finished. Even when it wasn't my day to cook. I had met a lot of interesting people and I'd learned why dogs were considered man's best friend. Of course, some of the dogs weren't man's best friend, either.

You don't expect a cute little dog like a Chihuahua to bite, do you? I know I didn't. But Mrs. Springer's Chihuahua was the meanest little thing I ever saw. He reminded me of Blossom before I started walking her.

I had always expected Blossom to be mean and vicious, but she was as gentle as a lamb. Looks sure can be deceiving. Like with Catriona Maryland. If I had been that girl, I wouldn't've come to Teena's birthday dinner.

But Catriona did show up.

All that came at the end of the week. First I have to tell about Mrs. Springer's Chihuahua. That evening, about a quarter after six, I'd already walked the last of the dogs I'd had for that day. I'd opened the kitchen door and Mama'd handed me the message Mrs. Springer had left.

"She's frantic," Mama said. "She fell down the steps a month ago and needs somebody to walk her little dog. Call her back and let her know if you can do it today."

I plopped down into a kitchen chair, dialed Mrs. Springer, and told her I'd be right over.

"Her dog's name is Buffo," I told Mama as I hung up the phone. "Sounds like a clown." I laughed and went out the back door.

Mrs. Springer was in the backyard sunning herself and reading the evening paper when I got there. Her left leg was in a cast.

Buffo was hardly bigger than a can of pop. I bet my father could've hidden the little dog in his cupped hands.

"You don't need to stay out with him too long,"

Mrs. Springer said. "Fifteen or twenty minutes is long enough. You can walk him again tomorrow when there's more time."

"Yes," I said. Buffo was tethered to one of the posts on the clothesline. I went to get him.

Before I got halfway, the little dog leapt up on me, sinking his claws into my bare thigh. "Ouch!" I yelled.

Mrs. Springer got off the chaise lounge and hobbled over to me. "Are you okay, Miranda?"

Buffo leapt up again and sank his teeth in the rough fabric of my cut-off jeans.

"I'm okay. I think he just wants to get out," I said.

"Maybe so, but he's not going to attack you like that." To Buffo she said, "You behave yourself." She wagged a finger at the little dog. He sat on his haunches, looking at her like he understood exactly what she was saying. He stared up at her with those great big sad eyes of his.

I felt sorry for him.

"You don't have to worry, Miranda. He's going to be very good, or else."

Mrs. Springer had been right. Buffo was on his best behavior as we circled the block.

When I got him home again, he curled up on the edge of the chaise lounge beside Mrs. Springer and was sound asleep before she could unpin the leash from his collar.

"Oh, that's so much nicer," Mrs. Springer said

as she took her change purse out of her slacks pocket and handed me some bills. "Thank you so much, Miranda."

"You're welcome," I said.

When I got home, I stuck the money in the vase on my desk where I kept pens and pencils. Sitting to my desk to rest before changing, I was really glad Mama and Daddy would be at the party, too, so I could feed them. The day of Teena's party was my day to cook. I wasn't about to cook two separate meals in one day.

By the time Mama called me to supper, I was soaking in the tub, hoping it'd make me feel less tired. It almost worked, too. I'd promised to treat Teena to a movie as part of her birthday gift from me. I wanted to make sure she was free for her party on Friday. I was meeting Teena at Delightful Catering. We hadn't decided what movie to see. We were going to Monroeville Mall, to the Quadraplex.

I got out of the tub, toweled myself off, and put on blue slacks and a red plaid blouse. I crammed a lightweight sweater into my purse. Last time I'd gone to the movies the air conditioner had been up too high and I'd nearly froze. I wasn't letting that happen again.

It was almost six-thirty when I went out to the kitchen.

"You can eat if you want to," Mama said.

"I'll wait for Daddy. Besides, I'm supposed to take Teena to the movies today."

"Oh, you told me this morning. I'll wait for your father, too."

" 'Bye, Mama," I said, and left for Delightful Catering.

"Teena around here somewhere," Aunt Delight told me. "I'll see if I can find her. Sit down, make yourself comfortable."

Aunt Delight was in her office off from the kitchen. She got up and went to look for Teena. I took a seat at the table opposite where she'd sat. Propping my arm on the table, I nearly knocked over a pile of balled-up pieces of paper. There was a clean sheet she'd just started to scribble on.

Shortly, Aunt Delight came back. "Teena'll be along in a minute of two."

"Okay," I said.

Aunt Delight sat down again and started back to scribbling on the sheet of paper. Before she'd written more than a couple of words, she balled up the sheet and added it to the pile on her right.

She shook her head. "I don't know, Miranda. I've been trying to come up with something catchy for my newspaper ad for the past week or two. What this needs is a fresh brain, I guess." She shook her head again. A few strands of salt-

and-pepper hair fell out from under her hair net. She wrote on the page again. This time, she didn't ball it up. She held it up, studied it. "Read this." She handed the sheet to me. I took it.

I read it and said, "It's nice." That was all I could think to say. I thought it needed more zip, or something.

"Well, jot down something. Anything that comes to mind." Aunt Delight handed me her pen. It was an old-fashioned fountain pen with a blue barrel and a silver cap. I took it. I had no idea what to write on the paper.

I stared at what Aunt Delight had written. She'd wanted to focus on how good the food was at Delightful Catering.

All I could think of was, "Food is always good when somebody else do the cooking." Although I'd been saying that a long, long time, I'd never had reason to write it down before. I scribbled it on the piece of paper, then crossed out "some-body else" and wrote in "Delightful Catering."

I slid the paper over to Aunt Delight just as Teena came out of a back room.

"All set?" Teena said.

"Let's go." I got up. "I'll see you later," I told Aunt Delight.

Outside on the sidewalk I told Teena, "My mother had nerve enough to want me to be friendly with Catriona."

"Catriona Maryland?" Teena asked. She looked

at me, stretching her eyes in disbelief.

"I hope there isn't another one out there some-where."

We walked along silently, headed for the bus stop. Leaves from the trees planted along the sidewalk had already started falling. We stepped on some crunchy gold ones as we stepped off the curb and crossed the street.

"You know," I said. "I've always thought Catriona's name sounds like a city and a state. A small town in Maryland."

Teena laughed.

"Catriona's job is over," Teena said.

"I know."

We were at the bus stop. A breeze had come up. It was blowing my hair all around my head. I kept pushing the hair away from my face. The breeze wasn't enough to do anything about the heat. But it was making my eyes smart a little because of my new contact lenses.

"Be sure to come to dinner on Saturday night," I told Teena.

"I'll be there. I wouldn't miss eating some of your cooking."

I couldn't tell her Catriona was going to be there, too. Might spoil her appetite. I changed the subject. "You know, I bet I've walked dogs from almost every country in the world."

Teena laughed again. "I know. If you stay in business long enough, you probably will."

"Tomorrow morning, I'm going to walk a Saint Bernard."

Our bus came. We got on and found a seat together near the middle of the bus. We made ourselves comfortable for the long ride to the Monroeville Mall and the movies.

TWENTY-FOUR

On Saturday, Daddy was too busy to mow the lawn, so while the chocolate cake I'd baked for Teena cooled on the kitchen table, I went out and cut the grass.

At first, I could still smell the chocolate cake, then partway through the mowing, I started smelling only cut grass. It smelled ripe, fresh, clean — like green fruit.

I got the leaf rake out of the garage and raked all the loose blades of grass, bagged it up, and put it back into the garage with the rake.

By the time I'd washed up and gone back to the kitchen, the cake was cool enough to frost and decorate. I used a tube of soft yellow icing to write HAPPY BIRTHDAY, TEENA and trim the edges of the cake. It looked almost good as if the professionals at a bakery had baked the cake. Not bad for a beginner, I thought.

I left the cake on the counter so the letters and the trim could harden. Then I went upstairs, took a shower, and changed. I put on white pants with pleats and three pockets, and a white T-shirt. I pulled on a long-sleeved red-and-white-striped blouse over the T-shirt.

Then, after twirling in front of the long mirror behind the closet door in Mama's room, I went downstairs and started making sure everything was set up the way I wanted it.

I think it was just like Mama said. Catriona was a lonely young girl. She was the first to show up for Teena's birthday dinner. She strolled in just as I was rubbing two sticks together to see if I could still make a fire without a match. I could. Catriona had stood there watching, fascinated.

"Looks like you learned a lot in camp," she said, and smiled. "You'll have to teach me that trick."

"Maybe," I said, still unsure if I could trust Catriona. She hadn't gone back and told on me at Produceland like she'd threatened. I think that's all she was. Full of threats. I guess looks can be deceiving. Look at Blossom. I'd always thought she was the most dangerous and vicious dog in the world, but she wasn't. From walking her almost daily, I found out she'd just wanted to play.

When the coals started glowing in the barbecue grill, I put the grate on it so it could get hot. It was smoking just a little bit now. I stood staring at Catriona. Maybe she did seem friendlier. I do know one thing, I was still going to keep one eye open when I was around her.

Kids started coming one at a time, then the yard was suddenly filled with them. It looked like more than the ten kids I'd invited. One of Teena's CDs was still in the little red stereo. I turned it on. Music filled the yard.

Teena came through the gate. I went to meet her.

"You didn't tell me you were having a party," she said.

"It isn't. It's just a dinner." Teena was dressed like me, but her striped shirt was dark blue. She glanced over at Catriona. She didn't say anything. "It's part of my campaign to be nice to Catriona, or Catey, as her mother calls her."

Teena smiled. She went to the punch bowl on the picnic table and helped herself to punch.

I went upstairs and got one of Teena's CDs. There was a particular song that I liked. Although I'd brought a few of the CDs downstairs, there was still a giant stack on the chest of drawers and on the floor in my room. I found the CD I was looking for and went back outside.

"The host shouldn't run out on her guests," Teena said as I got ready to change the CD.

"Got to keep the good music going," I said, and laughed.

"My mother's picking me up later. She's bringing some boxes and I'm taking my CDs home."

Before I could say anything, Brian Waters tapped Teena on the shoulder. He took her hand and led her onto the patio and they started dancing. Catriona was already dancing with Tony Wood. Only showing off would be a better description of what she was doing. Most of the other kids were just standing around watching them. They were gyrating and sashaying around the patio, and singing with the record like they were a rock and roll duo up for a Grammy award or something.

The rest of the kids stood on the sidelines laughing and clapping to the beat. I went and joined them.

After the song ended, I put hot dogs and hamburgers on the grill. Then I put my favorite song on the CD, and lots of other kids started dancing.

I tended the food. When the food was done, I brought out the baked beans. I had had them simmering on the kitchen stove, and they were good and hot.

While my favorite song filled the air, we ate dinner.

Later, Catriona surprised me by clearing away the paper dishes. I still can't believe it.

I brought out the birthday cake, plopped it on a corner of the table, and handed Teena the knife. I turned the volume down on the stereo.

While I got things ready, everybody huddled on one corner of the patio, including Mama and Daddy.

Just then, Mr. and Mrs. Shephard stuck their heads out of their back door. "Come on over," I said to them.

They came over. Blossom climbed up on the fence, her front paws gripping the top of it. Looked like she wanted to come over, too.

"Mr. Shephard, Mrs. Shephard, look here," my father said.

I had no idea what they were planning. I looked at them; they were all huddled together like football players planning strategy or something. I went back into the kitchen and got paper plates. I put a stack next to the cake. I struck a match and lighted the candles. "Okay, Teena, it's all yours."

Teena left the crowd and came to the table. She picked up the knife.

Brian Waters said, "Okay, everybody, hit it!"

We sang, "Happy birthday to you. Happy birthday, dear Teena. And many mo-o-o-re!"

At the back of the crowd, somebody said, "How old are you?"

Someone else — I think it was Catriona — said, "Count the candles, you idiot!"

We laughed.

"Make a wish," I told Teena.

Teena covered her face with her hands and made a wish, then blew out the candles. She got them all at the same time.

Catriona said, "What you wish for?"

"I'll never tell. Then it might not come true."

I took the candles out of their little yellow candy candle holders and put them on a paper plate. Teena cut the cake.

Earlier, when I'd started baking the cake, Mama, always the dietitian, had warned, "You better make a two-layer rectangular cake. It'll yield more slices."

I hadn't listened to her. I'd baked a three-layer round cake. Teena had to make awfully thin slices in order to have enough for everyone.

The CD had stopped. No music filled the air. Teena served cake all around.

Mama approached the table. Teena cut off a piece of cake with her fork, ate it, and said, "Now, Mrs. Moses?"

Mama grinned and said, "Now."

They all raised their voices and said, "FOOD IS ALWAYS GOOD WHEN MIRANDA DO THE COOKING!"

We laughed.

"Thanks," I said softly, smiling to myself.

Everybody clapped and we finished eating cake.

While I ate, I thought about going to Produce-land on Sunday after church and getting Mama a brand-new suspense thriller. Right after I got through walking the dogs.

ABOUT THE AUTHOR

JOHNNIECE MARSHALL WILSON made her writing debut with Scholastic Hardcover with *Oh, Brother,* which was an IRA/Children's Choice for 1989, and published her second book, *Robin on His Own,* with Scholastic Hardcover in 1990. Ms. Wilson lives with her three daughters in Wilkinsburg, Pennsylvania, and works at St. Francis Medical Center. She is currently at work on a new book.

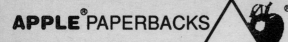

APPLE® PAPERBACKS

Pick an Apple and Polish Off Some Great Reading!

BEST-SELLING APPLE TITLES

❏ MT43944-8	**Afternoon of the Elves** Janet Taylor Lisle	**$2.75**
❏ MT43109-9	**Boys Are Yucko** Anna Grossnickle Hines	**$2.95**
❏ MT43473-X	**The Broccoli Tapes** Jan Slepian	**$2.95**
❏ MT40961-1	**Chocolate Covered Ants** Stephen Manes	**$2.95**
❏ MT45436-6	**Cousins** Virginia Hamilton	**$2.95**
❏ MT44036-5	**George Washington's Socks** Elvira Woodruff	**$2.95**
❏ MT45244-4	**Ghost Cadet** Elaine Marie Alphin	**$2.95**
❏ MT44351-8	**Help! I'm a Prisoner in the Library** Eth Clifford	**$2.95**
❏ MT43618-X	**Me and Katie (The Pest)** Ann M. Martin	**$2.95**
❏ MT43030-0	**Shoebag** Mary James	**$2.95**
❏ MT46075-7	**Sixth Grade Secrets** Louis Sachar	**$2.95**
❏ MT42882-9	**Sixth Grade Sleepover** Eve Bunting	**$2.95**
❏ MT41732-0	**Too Many Murphys** Colleen O'Shaughnessy McKenna	**$2.95**

Available wherever you buy books, or use this order form.

Scholastic Inc., P.O. Box 7502, 2931 East McCarty Street, Jefferson City, MO 65102

Please send me the books I have checked above. I am enclosing $_____ (please add $2.00 to cover shipping and handling). Send check or money order — no cash or C.O.D.s please.

Name_____ **Birthdate**_____

Address _____

City_____ **State/Zip** _____

Please allow four to six weeks for delivery. Offer good in the U.S.A. only. Sorry, mail orders are not available to residents of Canada. Prices subject to change.

APP693